SEDUCED

Beau Reve Series Book 1

Elissa Daye

World Castle Publishing, LLC
Pensacola, Florida
Copyright © Elissa Daye 2020
Hardcover ISBN: 9798378142538
Paperback ISBN: 9781951642327
eBook ISBN: 9781951642334
First Edition World Castle Publishing, LLC, February 10, 2020
http://www.worldcastlepublishing.com
Licensing Notes
Cover: Melissa Davis
Editor: Maxine Bringenberg

Chapter 1

"Watch out for table three. They're ass grabbers," warned Amelia.

"Good to know." Tara was not looking forward to taking over Amelia's shift, but what choice did she have? Someone had to pay the bills, and while she didn't like working at the night club, it paid decent on the weekends.

"They don't pay me enough for this shit." Candy rolled her eyes as she straightened her skirt, trying to get it to stay in place. "Bachelor party from hell."

"You'd think Lane ran a strip club," sighed Tara.

"He might as well, considering the outfit he makes us wear." Amelia gestured to the black skirt and tight pink tank top that was cut two inches too low. "That's why they come here. It's cheaper than the strip club. We should charge them for every time they touch us."

"If only. They don't even tip well." Tara rolled her eyes.

"Lane never does anything about it."

"He needs to hire a bouncer, like yesterday," complained Lola.

"And cut into the profits?" Amelia shook her head, derisively. "Ain't never gonna happen."

"Ladies! There are thirsty patrons. Less chit-chat. Lou, did you water the whiskey down?"

Lou barely looked up. "Yeah, boss."

"Good, good." He rubbed his hands together. "Back to work, ladies."

Tara watched him leave and looked over at Amelia. "Enjoy your break."

"Break, ha—the whole ten minutes? Maybe I should take up stripping."

"You already do enough of it outside of here anyway," teased Lola.

"Hey, that's for fun, not for the money." Amelia winked at Lola.

"Right...I believe you." Candy winked back.

"Girls, she's a sex addict. Paying her would only be a bonus." Tara couldn't help herself.

"At least I get some." Amelia wrinkled her nose at Tara.

"Oh, I get mine," Tara added. It was a total lie, but no one called her out on it.

"Ladies, you better get back out there before Lane blows a gasket. You remember what happened last time."

"He took our tips," grumbled Lola.

"Asshole," complained Candy.

"Yes, but that asshole cuts your paycheck and mine." Lou nodded over to where the self-satisfied owner was chatting with a pretty brunette.

"Off to serve the ass grabbers. Wish me luck," muttered Tara as she tugged her skirt down further.

"Girl, it won't matter how far you pull it down, it's still going to ride up your ass," teased Lola.

"I know, but a girl has to try. One day I'm going to wear spanks underneath. At least then they won't see my lady bits."

Amelia spit out her drink. "Vagina, Va-gi-na...girl, call it proper."

Tara shook her head and walked away. She didn't mind Amelia teasing her. The pretty blonde was actually the only real friend she had. Lola and Candy, they just tolerated Tara. Tara was kind of used to that. Lola and Candy were two of the most popular waitresses there, probably because their breasts were stripper sized. Tara sometimes wondered if they were natural, but she didn't make it a point to stare too long. It was bad enough that the men did that.

Tara walked over to Amelia's table. "Gentleman, your drinks."

"Aww, where'd the blonde go?" One of the men asked her. He looked a little bit like a bear, huskier than the other two.

"She's on break. Don't worry, I'll take good care of

you." Tara placed the drinks on the table.

"Oh, will you now?" The bear pulled her into his lap and tried to feel up her chest. He whispered into her ear, "If you're really good, we'll make sure to tip you real nice now."

"Well, that's certainly kind of you." She gave him a nice smile and carefully dislodged herself from his lap. "If you'll excuse me, Lou needs me to bring out another order."

"Come back soon, darling." He swatted her ass with his hand, hard enough for it to sting.

Tara's face was red when she went to the bathroom. She took in a few breaths and heard the door open behind her. Tara turned to the sound, half afraid one of those men had followed her into the bathroom.

"You all right, kid?" Lola asked her with concern.

"Fine. Same story, different night." Tara sighed. Men…. Let her rephrase that. Drunk men seemed to think the servers were objects to do with whatever they pleased. Tara wished she could smash her fist into his face, but that would make her lose her job.

"Make sure Lou really waters down their drinks next time. Maybe you could spit in their beer. It's foamy enough they'd never notice."

Tara giggled. "That's disgusting."

"Yeah, but that prick deserves it." Lola smiled at her and offered her a wet paper towel to cool her face.

"Thanks, Lola."

"Any time. We better get back out there. Lane's really cracking the whip tonight. The club's hopping."

"Of course, it is." She quickly wiped her face and shook it off. Time to get back to it. She only had three more hours of this crap to deal with. Only...heaven help her.

Tara returned out to the bar and saw the men at the table were leaving. Had someone answered her prayer? She walked over to clear their table and was disappointed that they had only left her a two-dollar tip. Hell, if she was being frisked at a strip club, she'd get a lot more money. That guy practically had a lap dance. It wasn't even worth keeping. She'd just hand it off to Amelia since she had spent the majority of their visit with them.

The next few hours were filled with even more obnoxious men, some with women who were ignoring their crass behavior. Why did women let their men act like that? They deserved a hell of a lot better. No man had the right to put his hands on another woman without their permission. That message was still not sinking into the world around her. That was probably why Tara didn't have much luck. That, and the fact that she was too busy working her ass off just to make ends meet. That was life, though.

When Tara was done with her shift, she walked out to her car in the well-lit parking lot. She had her keys positioned between each finger, just in case some schmuck decided to make a move on her. It was two in the morning, just the right time for the creeps to come out and play.

She quickly unlocked her door and slid inside, shivering slightly from the cold air. Locking her doors, she started the engine. Tara had never been attacked, but the fear was always there no matter how hard she tried to bury it deep inside her.

She made her way home as quickly as possible. When she pulled into the driveway, she saw a package on her porch. "Hmmm...mail must have come late today. Figures."

Tara never knew when the mail was going to arrive. Half the time, it was for her brothers, who no longer lived there. Tara pressed the button to the garage door and drove her car inside. She went outside to retrieve the package, then went back inside the garage. Closing the garage, she let herself into her house.

"Hmm...I'm slightly curious, but I really need a shower." Not because she smelled so much, but because she didn't like the dirty hands that had mauled her all evening. Her shift started at six o'clock. That was close to eight hours of sweaty drunks. She shivered.

After washing away the sweat and grit of the day, Tara slid into her cotton robe and sighed. There was something about a nice long shower followed with a fluffy robe. Wrapping her hair in a small towel, she finally made her way to the box on the table. Checking the address again, she reassured herself that the package was indeed hers. "Weird. I didn't order anything."

Tara put a hand on it and smirked. Several ideas

popped into her head at once. A secret admirer? A bomb? A decapitated head? "Maybe I watch too much TV. What is Beau Reve?" she wondered aloud. The package and letter had come from there. From the looks of the logo, Tara almost thought it was some kind of law firm. Maybe someone had sent her a present from them. Her brothers, perhaps?

Tracing her fingers over the envelope, she was still perplexed. The lettering certainly looked official. She slid a fingernail under the edge on one side and ripped it from corner to corner. "Congratulations, you've won a million dollars," she chuckled to herself. Like she'd ever be that lucky. Dare to dream, though, right?

Pulling out the letter inside, Tara almost held her breath. The logo appeared at the top, much like the envelope. Was this some kind of summons? Beau Reve, all-expense-paid two-week vacation...was she in an alternate dimension? There had to be some catch. Overpriced plane tickets? She had to buy a timeshare? That one had actually been pulled on her twice before. Like an underpaid waitress could afford a timeshare. That sure didn't stop them from trying to get whatever they could out of her.

"Like hell." She set the letter down, only half-reading it. Tara rolled her eyes. Was it even worth finishing? "Not like I have anything better to do, I guess." She picked the letter back up and read to the next page. She had been nominated for the vacation, but it didn't say by who. "Interesting."

Somehow she found it hard to believe. The list of people who could have nominated her for this was very short. In fact, one person came to mind. Tara picked up her phone and dialed the number, and groaned when she got her voicemail. "Amelia, did you nominate me for a vacation? I just got a letter in the mail. Call me when you get off work."

All expenses. That's what the letter stated. There was a twenty-four-hour helpline. Tara dialed the number and waited for someone to answer on the other end. She tapped her finger on the kitchen counter absently, and almost jumped when the operator on the other end picked up.

"Beau Reve, where your fantasies come alive. How may I assist you today?"

Fantasies? What was this, Disney World? She giggled despite herself. "Sorry. Um, Yeah, I got a package in the mail from your resort."

"Can you give me the number on the top?" The woman asked her.

"23798727." Tara bit her lip as she waited for the woman to respond.

"Ms. Hart?" The woman verified.

"Tara Hart, yes." This was getting more interesting by the moment.

"Wonderful, Ms. Hart. It looks like you've got a credit for a two-week vacation. When would you like to schedule it?"

"Excuse me?" She asked incredulously. "What's the

catch?"

"No catch," the woman tried to assure her.

"You're not trying to sell me anything? No timeshares? No vacation packages?" Tara ran her nail across the counter and tried to scrape some of the grime away. God, when was the last time she'd cleaned this counter? She quickly retrieved a wet cloth and waited to hear what mumbo jumbo the women would tell her next.

"We're not that kind of resort, Ms. Hart. We give away vacations all the time at Beau Reve, and we're happy to do it. Now, your stay includes all the amenities. Food, drink, entertainment. We even have our own transportation for you from your airport to our resort. Do you have any dates in mind?"

Tara nibbled on her bottom lip. "Any idea who might have nominated me for this vacation?"

"All nominations are anonymous. If you check the package that came along with it, you have airplane tickets with an open reservation on the top."

"I'm finding this a little difficult to believe." Tara tapped a finger on her counter.

"That's understandable. If you aren't ready to book your date now, you can use your identification number to set up your stay." The woman read off the script; she must have read a million times.

"Thank you. I need some time to think this over."

"We're here to help. Any day or night. Feel free to call

with any other questions you might have, Ms. Hart, and have a lovely night."

Tara heard the click of the phone on the other end and sighed. What a load of horse shit! There was no way they were going to hand her an all-expenses-paid trip. Like that ever happened.

Tara rubbed her temples and opened her fridge to find something to eat. Her mind was starting to race as she heated up her leftover pasta. A free vacation. That would be nice. She actually had saved up enough time to get away for two weeks, but that didn't mean Lane would let her out for that long. If she went, Tara would have to find someone willing to work those hours.

Tara sighed. She could use the vacation to get her mind off her worries if that were possible. Her life had been filled with worry and responsibility since the moment her parents had died, leaving her to raise her teenage brothers. Tara had been nineteen at the time and barely making her way through college. She dropped out to become their guardian and had been in survival mode ever since.

At one time, Tara had been working four jobs to get them through. Now that the boys had moved on to the next stage in their lives, Tara was thinking of selling their house. The money from the sale could help fund the last two years of Clay's college, and some could be set aside for Eric for when he got home from deployment. The boys hadn't wanted her to do that. Their house was filled with memories. Some good, some bad, but memories would carry with them no matter where they went.

Tara had planned on using her vacation time to clear out the house and find an apartment, but there was also a large part of her that was reluctant to let go of it. Tara passed by the picture of her brother Eric, and a tear filled her eye. She didn't like him being so far away, but he had been a self-proclaimed soldier all the way back in the day when he was playing with his tiny little plastic soldiers. Her grandfather had been in the military and lived through two wars. He was probably the reason why Eric had been so adamant.

"Oh, Tara. Girl, you got to get out of your head," she sighed.

Tara opened her laptop and typed in the website for Beau Reve. When it opened in her browser window, she saw a beautiful white sandy beach and palm trees. Was it near the tropics? She scrolled through all the pictures and amenities provided. Beau Reve looked like paradise, but there was one catch. As she read the catch line again, she had a feeling that something wasn't quite on the up and up with it. Where your fantasies come alive.

As she scrolled through some of the photos, she found an event calendar. Mixers, social events, massages, entertainers. Then there was a list of the different areas. At the bottom of the screen, she saw text in the tiniest of print. *All sexual encounters are consensual.*

"Say what now?" What kind of place was Beau Reve? A sexual fantasy island? She must be imagining things. At least she thought she was until she pulled the FAQ up.

"Can I have sex in public? Is there a dungeon? What kind of clothing should I bring?" Tara's cheeks started to feel hot. "Sex. Wow, they just put it all right out there, don't they?"

The next question actually made her feel better. "I've won a vacation, but I don't want to have sex. Can Beau Reve still be for me?"

Tara read the answers. Yes, while Beau Reve caters to the sexual desires of women, they need not participate in any of the activities in order to have a fulfilling time at Beau Reve. There is never any pressure to do anything that makes any woman uncomfortable. Well, that answered that question. So, the only question now was, could Tara go to Beau Reve, knowing what its covenant stood for?

Tara could count on one hand the number of vacations she'd had over the past six years. Zero. Not a one. Now that she was down to just one job, with vacation that would soon disappear if she didn't use it by the end of the year, the temptation was real. Tara decided not to make a decision until she talked to Amelia. Her friend was the only ear she trusted. Hopefully, she would call her back soon.

Chapter 2

Tara knew that Amelia would be getting home soon. Her shift was over at three, when they took the last call for the night. Their job was never done, it seemed. Tara made herself a quick sandwich and grabbed a bag of chips. It was late to eat, but Tara had more than worked off her dinner.

Tara plopped down on her bed and started to thumb through the cable stations. She finally found one of the CSI shows and started to watch it. As the detectives started to dissect a maggot, Tara swallowed a bite of her sandwich. Good thing she had an iron stomach. If not, she would have spat the food out. She was too hungry to care at this point.

"Damn it." She'd forgotten her water. Tara did not relish getting back out of bed. Her feet were throbbing painfully from the high heels she had to wear every night. She'd like to see Lane prance around in a pair of those sometime. He'd fall on his ass in the first two minutes.

Sighing, Tara set her food aside and went back out to the kitchen to get a bottle of water and a few cookies. Better to do it now, because she was going to want them in a few minutes and she'd just have to get right back up and get them. Best to cut that off at the pass. At least, that's what she told herself as she slid back onto her bed.

The coroner on the show started to slice open the cadaver just as her cell started to ring. She picked it up and wasn't surprised to see Amelia's number. She was right on time. "Girl, you're not going to believe what came in the mail today."

"So, you got it?"

"If you mean a letter from someplace called Beau Reve, then yes. Did you know about this?"

Tara crossed her arm over her chest. While it did bring some validity to the whole experience, she was a little perturbed that her friend would do something like this without telling her. Amelia must have had a good reason, though, because she told Tara everything—literally, *everything,* and sometimes in more detail than anyone really wanted to know. Like how big the man she was sleeping was, what he did with his tongue, if he snored, how long he lasted, and many, many other mundane things. Tara wasn't entirely sure why she shared as much as she did. Sometimes she'd throw her arms over her head, her signal that Amelia was oversharing, but that never seemed to stop her.

"Well, yes, in a way, but it wasn't me who put you in for it."

"Who did?" Tara nibbled on her bottom lip. She wracked her brains, trying to figure out who could have possibly put her name in for this vacation.

"Some guy who came to the bar one night. Apparently, he saw you being hassled by a table of jackasses, and was impressed with the way you handled yourself." Amelia sounded like she was smiling even from here.

"That's not all, though, is it?" That was never it. Amelia always led with just a little bit of information before throwing even more out there.

"Not quite. He was quite handsome, though. When he told me where he wanted to send you, I about had a heart attack."

"He probably thinks he can have his way with me." Tara put her head in her hands and shook it slowly. How in the world could she go there knowing some stranger thought she needed to get laid? And the fact that her best friend had been in on it in any shape or form made the joke that much crueler. And what did she mean, where he wanted to send her? "Do you know what Beau Reve is?"

"Yep. I've been there. Twice." Amelia's voice was envious. "Of course, I only got a week. I must not be a good girl. You're going to have a lot of fun."

"When was this?" Tara was now curious. When was the last time she'd seen Amelia take a vacation? Like ever?

Amelia was the only other person she knew who worked as hard as she did. Especially considering the years of college she still had to achieve to get her doctorate.

"It was two years ago before you started working at the bar. Two separate weeks of ecstasy. I'm almost jealous."

"Amelia, I can't go to some sexual fantasy island. It's not my thing." Tara pulled the covers closer to her legs as if to demonstrate how straight-laced she was, not that Amelia could see her. Tara had enough trouble walking about in a short skirt and high heels around the club's patrons. How in the world was she going to hook up with strangers? Not likely to ever happen in this century.

"You never know unless you try, Tara. Besides, you don't have to do anything. Just go and relax."

True. She could just relax if that were actually in her vocabulary. Sometimes Tara wished she had a pause button. "Where is it?"

"It's at an undisclosed location, to give its visitors privacy. An island in the tropics somewhere. No one will even know you went."

"You will."

Tara wasn't sure she wanted to be Amelia's punchline any time soon. If she did end up having some kind of island affair, Tara would never be able to live it down. *Ever!* She shook her head and sighed loudly.

"Well, yes. And I will want the details, of course. But your secret will be safe with me. Trust me, you'll love it there."

"Says you, Amelia. You and I, we're two different people." Sometimes Tara wished she could be a little more like Amelia, but life was too complicated for that.

"We're not so different. Just because I find sex to be something beneficial to my own personal sanity doesn't make me that different than you. Besides, I know where you keep your secret stash," Amelia teased her. "Do you need some batteries, Tara?"

"Amelia!" Tara turned red and tried to ignore the embarrassment flooding through her. Clearly, she was going to have to come up with a better hiding place. Sure, she'd taken care of herself from time to time. She was human, after all, and her body still had needs.

"You won't need toys at Beau Reve, Tara. And it's like Vegas — what happens there, stays there."

"Is that why you never told me about it before?" Tara asked her. She thought she knew all of Amelia's past sexual escapades. Her friend often shared them with her just to make her blush. If she went, she'd have a red face around Amelia for the rest of her life. Amelia would probably start to regale her with all her own stories, all while trying to drag any information from Tara.

"Well, I also didn't want to ruin the surprise. I was pretty sure my added recommendation would seal the deal. You have to go, Tara. Just think, a tropical paradise with anything your heart desires, even if it's just to catch up on your sleep."

"But it's not like I can just skip out on work." Which was true. Paying her bills was something Tara had to do. She didn't believe in letting a single bill go, even if they gave her an extension. That messed with your credit score, after all. Credit she wasn't even using, but still. Even though she had vacation time, she'd still have to convince Lane to give her the time.

"About that.... Yes, you can. I've already gotten the girls onboard. We're more than happy to take any of your shifts while you're gone. We all could use the money."

"Amelia! Oh my god, did you tell everyone else?" Tara could not keep the mortification out of her voice. If any of the others knew, she might have to quit. Amelia made fun of her in private, but the ladies.... They meant well, but their words could sometimes come out the wrong way. They didn't have the same insecurities that she had.

"Relax. The girls only know that you have an opportunity for a vacation. Besides, you've done them all a solid any time they needed it. They're willing to help you out."

"What if my vacation hours aren't enough to pay my bills, Amelia?" She was making a mental calculation in her head. Missing hours didn't cover the missed tips. The tips were what kept her afloat most weeks.

"About that. Did you find anything else in the envelope?"

"Not that I know of. Let me check." Tara jumped out of bed and retrieved the envelope. In her hurry to read the letter, Tara could have missed something. She pulled out a smaller slip of paper and almost lost her mind. "Twenty thousand dollars? Are you shitting me?"

"So, you did get it. Good. I knew you would worry about your bills. They promised me that they would take care of it."

Her friend seemed a little anxious on the other end. What was she hiding from her? Nothing was free. It never was.

"Who? Who are they?" *What kind of place pays for people to be off work and gives them a free vacation?* Her doubts swarmed in her head like hundreds of bees in a mason jar. Tara couldn't hold onto one thought long enough to think. She rubbed her head as her mind raced.

"Beau Reve. They have funds in place for situations like these." Amelia sounded secretive, and Tara didn't like it one bit.

"Situations like these? What are you holding back, Amelia?" Tara nibbled on her bottom lip, waiting to find out what Amelia could be holding back from her.

"It may or may not be an exotic lonely-hearts club."

"Wait. What? I'm not going then. I don't need to be fixed up with anyone, Amelia. I can do just fine on my own, thank you."

Exotic lonely-hearts club? There wasn't an exotic bone

21

in Tara's body. Surely Amelia knew that. Her dream date was dinner and a movie. Sex never really entered into it. Now, if a man was around long enough and put in the time, then perhaps there might be sex. At twenty-five, though, most of the men she met were only interested in sex, so it was kind of a deal-breaker for both sides.

"That's not what Eric said."

"What the hell! You've been conspiring with my brother?" Tara shook her head at the phone. If Amelia had been there, she would have taken her friend by the shoulders and given her a good shake. She settled for a stiff glare, which was clearly pointless, considering her friend couldn't see her. What the hell was she thinking, bringing her family into this?

"Both of them, actually. They want to see you happy. I want to see you laid."

"Amelia! You didn't say that to them, did you?"

It wasn't like Tara was a Puritan. She'd had a few relationships, and she certainly wasn't a naive virgin. True, she hadn't been with anyone in a little while, but that didn't mean she needed help in that department. Why did everyone seem to think they needed to meddle in her life? She never meddled in theirs.

What people seemed to forget was that one could survive without sex, especially in the age of technology. Trying to explain that to Amelia wouldn't go well since she had a new man every few weeks. Apparently, Amelia's

motto was, "Don't settle down until you've tried them all."
She even admitted it, much to Tara's chagrin. Tara had
never understood Amelia's reasoning, but then again, Tara
wanted to find someone to settle down with more than she
wanted to have fun. Unfortunately, most people her age
were only interested in sex. Tara had just turned twenty-
five, and while that would have seemed like a good age to
find men, it hadn't panned out at all.

"It wasn't me who brought that up, actually."

"Oh, dear lord." Tara felt her face start to burn as an
embarrassing flush lit her skin afire. Her brothers thought
she was a prude? What had she done wrong over the years
to deserve this? Had she not treated them fairly and helped
them figure out adolescence and how-to adult?

"Yeah, I was a little uncomfortable answering questions
about your personal life. Anyway, the point is, this resort
was founded to provide those with less the ability to explore
themselves at Beau Reve."

"I can explore myself just fine at home." Crap! Had
she just said that? Amelia's chuckle on the other end was
her answer. Tara felt a hot flush cover her face. "That's not
what I meant. I don't need to go to a sex resort, Amelia. It's
just not my thing."

"Look. Beau Reve is providing you with a much-needed
vacation. Take it, Tara."

"Amelia! I can't just—"

"You can and you will, or your brothers will have my

hide. They might even come knocking on your door. Maybe you'll meet a handsome stranger and have wild passionate sex; I hear they have special rooms for that there. I never did get to try those out."

"You're incorrigible. I'm not going, Amelia. It's not my thing." Sex rooms? What in the world was she talking about now? *Oh, good grief.* Tara thought her face had surpassed red and was starting to turn violet at this point. Could Amelia embarrass her anymore?

"How would you know? Live a little. What harm could it do? You don't have to do anything with anyone. You can sit by the pool and ignore the world around you. At least go and relax."

Why did Tara feel like Amelia was leaving something out? What kind of place was this Beau Reve? Did it really have sex rooms? At an exotic paradise? Was it a club med for horny rich people? Maybe a secret nudist colony? Tara could not help but imagine the worst.

"Bah. And if I say no?"

"Brotherly love comes knocking at your door—well, one of them. But the other will give you an earful on Skype."

"Oh, dear. They wouldn't…. Crap. Yes, they would."

Her brothers were ferocious when it came to her doing things for herself. Clearly, her lack of a real break in the past six years had not set well with them. It wasn't their fault that Tara was so well-adjusted and responsible. That had been in her character well before she'd taken on raising her brothers. It was just who Tara was. Maybe her life hadn't turned out the way she had wanted, but it was the only life she knew now.

Nevertheless, Tara knew she would be hounded until she went, so she really had only one choice. Bite the bullet. Go on the vacation. But she could still draw the line at how far she was willing to go while she was there. No one else would be there to bully her, and she could turn her phone off, so she didn't have to read any of their texts egging her on.

"Fine. I'll go. But I'm not getting laid, so get that out of your head right now."

"Uh-huh. Right. You're getting laid. Gotcha."

"You only hear what you want to hear, you know that?" Tara smiled in spite of herself. Amelia was set in her ways.

"So you keep saying. Now, get your crap packed and get it booked already. Did you open the box yet?"

"Uhm...no. Hold on."

Tara peeled back the tape at one side then ripped it away. When she opened the lid, Tara found it was filled with packing peanuts. She dug inside the box and found an envelope, a smaller box, and a small garment, which ended up being a two-piece bikini.

Opening the envelope, she found a letter that informed her that Beau Reve was in a tropical climate, which was why they sent her the complimentary suit. The open-ended airplane tickets were also inside the envelope. Tara opened the box and found a snow globe that fit in both her hands. Inside was a red lacy mask, what appeared to be a black feather, and some object that made no sense to her. Was that a whip? What the actual fuck? Maybe she should change her mind before it was too late. There was no way in hell she would let anyone whip her, or wield one for that matter.

"Did you get it?"

"Yeah. And some weird ass snow globe too." Tara shook her head and shuddered slightly as she set the globe on the counter.

"Who cares about the snow globe? Get your things packed. Call me when you've picked your date. You're lucky. You even get to check-in through the private terminal. Best transportation ever."

"Okay, Amelia. But if this goes south, you are never going to hear the end of it." Did she just say private terminal? Weren't those for the smaller jets? Private planes? That made sense if it was truly funded by billionaires. Tara wondered if their gifted vacations counted as a tax cut.

"Whatever, Tara. Just get some for a change, okay? Good night. Sweet dreams, Tara. Text me tomorrow."

"Fine."

Tara hung up the phone, and was half tempted to call her brothers to chew them out for their interference, but realized the more she didn't share with them the worse it would be for them. Let them stew in their curiosity. As much as she wanted to be furious with them, the truth of the matter was, she was a little in awe of their generosity. They had put time and effort into surprising her, something that they often did not have to spare. It made her heart feel full to be so loved.

Chapter 3

After much thought, several doubts, days of deliberation, and hounding from Amelia, Tara finally gave in and put in her request for vacation. She still had one more night of work before she was officially on vacation, and she was already dreading it. How many men would she have to keep off her tonight? And to think, Beau Reve might not be any better.

Tara sighed as she looked over her makeup in the restroom one last time. "Time to just bite the bullet."

She left the safety of the bathroom and planted a smile firmly on her face. There was no way she was going to let any of the regulars make her night a living hell. Not tonight. No sirree.

Tara walked to the bar and smiled at Lou. "Any orders in?"

"Not yet. Sure are going to miss you around here." He

nodded to her.

"Me? Pshaw. There's plenty of others here to fill my shoes."

"Yes, but you always get the orders right." He grinned at her.

"Just takes a little extra brainpower."

"You should have finished college."

"Who told you about that, Lou?" Tara shook her head slowly. "That was a lifetime ago."

"You can always go back. What were you studying?" He asked her curiously.

"Accounting."

Tara had wanted to be an accountant at one point. Math had always been her favorite subject. Maybe that's why she could tell how underpaid they were with their tips. Percentages were easy for her. Half the people who came here had no idea how to tip. Some left without even considering it. Tipping did not seem to be in their vocabulary. It wasn't just the millennials, either. Sometimes even the baby boomers forgot.

"You'd be good at that. At management too. I bet if Lou had a position open, he'd consider you. I'd recommend you in a heartbeat."

Tara laughed softly. "If I was managing this place, I'd make a lot of changes. First, I'd hire a bouncer. We should not have to put up with the handsy jerks that come in here. This should be an upscale joint."

"What else would you do?" He asked her curiously.

"Make designer drinks and signature cocktails. People go crazy for those things. Especially if we entered them in one of those competitions." Tara looked over at her tables that were starting to fill up. "Gotta go, Lou."

Tara walked to her first table and saw two couples. "Good evening. I'm Tara. How can I help you tonight?"

"Two waters and two beers," one of the men answered for them.

Tara looked at the women. One of them was not too happy. "Is that all?"

"Yes," the man replied.

"Coming right up."

Tara started to walk away and heard one of the women complain about not wanting water.

"I wanted a real drink, Al."

"Why should I buy you some overpriced drink? Especially considering the fact that I have more fun watching that girl's ass than playing tickle the pickle with you any day of the week.

"Al!" The woman was mortified.

Tara didn't feel that much better having heard the display. Why would any woman stay in that situation? She'd be far better off on her own than having a cretin. Unfortunately, women who chose to stay were hard to talk into leaving. Tara wouldn't get involved, even though she really wanted to.

Tara thought about what Lou had asked her. What would she do if she managed a club? Maybe cater to the women more than the men. Have a ladies' night with half-priced drinks? She'd make the club a little more upscale to bring in people who would actually tip appropriately. Many things came to mind, none of which Tara would ever voice to Lane. That man wouldn't hear her anyway. He was too used to the sound of his own voice to really listen to the rest of them.

The longer the night went on, the more Tara was starting to wish she had picked a different career path altogether. If she finished the last two years of college, maybe she'd have a much more lucrative career. Maybe she could take a class at a time. With the extra money from the check she had deposited in the bank, she might be able to afford one at a time.

Of course, maybe it would be better to use it to pay for her brother's schooling. Tara didn't want him to leave school with any loans — not if she could help it. Her parents had only saved enough for half of his tuition. That was quickly dwindling with the cost of books, room, and board. When Clay had offered to go to a community college and stay at home, Tara just couldn't let him do that. He should have the full college experience that would hopefully lead him to a wonderful career. If he could support himself, she wouldn't have to worry about it.

By the time Tara ended her shift, it was one in the

31

morning. She had wanted to get out of there earlier, but they had been short-staffed. She was going to leave early in the morning and had hoped to get more sleep, but that couldn't be helped now.

Tara made her way to the parking lot and saw a few men standing near the curb. She felt her heart race slightly and prayed that they didn't notice her. Luckily, they were too far gone to hear her small steps across the pavement. Tara quickly unlocked her car and got inside. She was starting to get afraid more and more each night. Maybe it was time to re-evaluate her life and find a job that didn't make her feel like she was fresh meat on a slaughtering block every night.

She drove home as fast as she could without breaking too many laws on the way. All she wanted to do was get a few hours of sleep before she had to get up. Thank goodness the roads were fairly empty tonight. That made her journey a lot less stressful.

When she pulled into her garage, she breathed a sigh of relief. Home at last. She got out of her car and closed the garage door. Time to pack her suitcase. Hopefully, that wouldn't take more than a half-hour. As excited as she should be, there was a fair amount of nervousness that went along with it. That nervousness was what had kept her from packing her things.

Tara went to her closet and pulled out the large suitcase that had once belonged to her mother. It had collected dust over the years, so she had to wipe it down before she opened it up. When her parents had passed away unexpectedly, she was barely out of high school and had become a responsible adult while the rest of her friends were out living their lives. Life had been a rollercoaster of debt and responsibility ever since. What else could she do but carry on the way she always had?

She quickly packed everything one might need in a tropical climate, all the while thinking about what it would be like to have nothing to do all day but sit on the beach. Tara even tracked down her passport just in case she needed it while she traveled. Even if a private jet were to touch down on a tropical island, there might be somewhere they checked passports. After she packed up the rest of her clothes, Tara realized that she was still standing around in her robe. Changing into her pajamas, she crawled into bed and made sure her alarm was on for the crack of dawn. Tomorrow was going to be a long day.

When the alarm woke her up in the morning, Tara jolted out of bed as if the house were on fire. Speaking of the house, Tara was glad Amelia had agreed to check on it while she was gone. Water mains, unexpected house fires, any of those things could happen while she was gone. Okay, so the likelihood was slim, but still, Tara had learned to be prepared for them nonetheless.

"Bags, check. Purse, check." Tara looked around to see if there was anything else she was missing. A honk sounded outside, and she sighed. "Right on time."

The cab driver hopped out of the car to help her with her bags. "Allow me, miss."

"Thank you." She smiled at him. Tara made a mental note to make sure he got a good review and a tip when she was done. She opened her door and slid inside.

When the cab driver started to make his way down the street, he gave her a big smile. "Vacation?"

"Yes, but my husband couldn't come with me." Tara didn't want the driver to think her house would be empty. "Police officer—hard to get away, you know."

"That's too bad. My brother's a cop. I know how grueling the hours can be."

"Definitely." Tara wrinkled her nose and looked out the window, hoping the driver wouldn't ask her too many more questions. She just wanted to get to the airport and get on her way.

The drive seemed to take forever, but in all actuality, it was less than half an hour to get there. The driver opened her door for her and then went back to retrieve her bags. "Have a wonderful vacation."

"Thank you, I think I will." Tara sent her payment to his console and gave him an extra twenty dollars.

He saw the dash and gave her a big smile. "That's awfully generous, miss."

"You deserve it. Not everyone can do what you do. Thank you." She offered him a smile, and he gave her a polite bow.

Tara pulled the handles on her luggage and made the trek into the airport. It was so huge she had no idea where she was going. Tara looked for the first official-looking person she could find. "Excuse me."

"How may I help you?" The older woman inquired.

"I'm looking for the Startlet terminal."

"Ah, yes. That's our private terminal. It's all the way past the United Airlines. When you get to the end of that one, you make a left, and it will lead you straight there."

"Thank you." Tara smiled at her.

"Have a wonderful trip," the woman wished her.

Tara may have been imagining things, but she could have sworn the guard had an extra twinkle in her eyes. Did she know Tara was heading to Beau Reve? Oh, God, she hoped not. Tara still couldn't believe that her brothers knew about her trip. She was never going to hear the end of it.

Amelia — she could see why she would be behind it any of it, even if it were instigated by some handsome stranger. Well, they were all in for a brutal awakening when Tara returned with no stories to tell. She'd sit on the beach and soak up some rays, but she wouldn't get caught up in whatever sexual fantasy they wished for her. Let them wonder just what happened — Tara would never tell.

Tara found the terminal easily and walked right up to the front desk. "Good morning, I have a nine o'clock flight."

"Ticket, please," the man asked her.

If he had any thoughts about her destination, he didn't share them. Thank goodness for that.

"How many bags? Just the one?"

"I decided to travel light." Tara had crammed as much as she could into that one suitcase, so if she didn't have it, she didn't need it. That was all there was to it.

"I'll take those for you. If you want to just have a seat, the plane seems to be on time."

"Thank you."

Tara looked for a place to sit and was surprised that she wasn't the only one there. There were two other women waiting to board as well. Neither one looked as apprehensive as she did.

The blonde turned to her and smiled. "First time?"

"I'm sorry?" Tara wasn't prepared for friendly conversation just yet.

"Is it your first time going to Beau Reve?"

"What makes you say that?" Did she have a scarlet letter pinned on her shirt somewhere?

"You look like you're about to go to a funeral. Do you remember when we took our first trip?" The blonde turned to the redhead.

"Yes. Of course, I think I was the one dragging you there at the time. Relax. I'm Sienna. This one here is Rachel."

"Tara."

That's all she wanted to say about that really, but the

women were obviously a chatty pair. She counted to ten in her head and reminded herself of the book she had brought to read on vacation. Just one flight away, and she would be in the sun diving into it. Patience.

"Well, Tara. What brings you to Beau Reve?" Sienna asked her.

Tara sighed and tried her best not to snap at the nosy women. "If you must know, I'm being sent against my will."

"Oh, that won't do at all." Rachel shook her head. "You should want to go. Why are you here, then?"

"I actually could use a vacation," Tara mumbled.

"Leave her alone, Rachel. If I remember correctly, I had to drag you too. Now you're the one dragging me this time."

"Like hell!" Rachel shook her head. "That girl practically lives there now."

"Is that even possible?" Tara looked at them in confusion. These women were frequent fliers? She would make sure to keep that from Amelia. If her friend knew that she could go all the time, Tara would never see her again. That, and she would get stuck covering all her shifts.

"You'll see, Tara. It's paradise, and the men there believe in pampering their women."

The men pamper the women? Tara hadn't known any men like that. Sure, she'd had an occasional date here and there where she had been taken out to dinner and maybe a movie, but none of them had stuck around long enough to start developing feelings for her. Maybe that was her fault, though. She hadn't had time for anything permanent, not unless that person had been willing to help support her family the way she had. Of course, now that her brothers were old enough to be financially responsible for themselves, Tara hadn't been able to use that excuse for quite some time.

"What if I just want to relax on the beach?"

"You'd be missing all the fun." Rachel shook her head in disbelief.

"Free country, or island." Sienna winked at her.

"Why is it free?"

"It's kind of a billionaire playground. They have money to spare," the redhead explained.

"And it's not just men paying. Some of them are women—if you like that flavor," teased Rachel.

"I see. Not particularly. Not that there's anything wrong with it." Tara crossed her legs in front of her and willed the chatty women to stop talking, which seemed to have no effect on them whatsoever.

"This is my fourth time. I've caught the eye of a few of the older crowd. Who knows, maybe I'll find a forever home this time with one of them." Rachel was clearly fantasizing. What was she, a puppy at the shelter looking for an owner?

Tara shook her head. Was that what Beau Reve was? Hunting grounds for husbands? Was that what the billionaires were looking for? Pliable women to mold to their own desires? They would sure be disappointed with Tara. She hadn't learned to bend for anyone. She'd never had the time for that kind of nonsense. It would take a lot more than money to make her that weak.

Tara was starting to think this was a bad idea. She was on the verge of leaving the small waiting area and heading back to her apartment when an attendant came to collect them. "Flight Beau Reve is ready to go. Follow me, ladies."

Tara stood and debated her options. If she went, she would probably have a lousy time. If she stayed here, she would never hear the end of it. Choices, choices. Tara took the leap and decided that Beau Reve couldn't be any more difficult than raising two teenage boys who constantly reminded her that she wasn't their mother. If she had survived all that crankiness, surely telling off a few billionaires would be easier. Her brothers had been absolute hell. This would be a piece of cake. She could always lock herself in her room and refuse to come out.

When they made their way onto the plane, Tara couldn't believe how swank it was. There were only six seats on the plane, all large like comfortable armchairs. Each seat had its own area with all the possible media one could need on a long trip. From the reading she had done, Beau Reve would take about eighteen hours to reach. At least they would be traveling in comfort.

Chapter 4

The moment the plane landed, Tara knew she was in a whole new world. They stepped off the plane into the most beautiful sunrise Tara had ever seen. The purples and pinks contrasted with the blue of the ocean and sand below. A white limo was making its way down the runway to meet them. When it pulled to a stop, a woman stepped out.

"Welcome to Beau Reve, my pets. I'm Kelli."

Pets? Uhm, what exactly was she talking about? Tara eyed her skeptically, but the other two women ran over and took turns throwing hugs around Kelli. Tara tried not to roll her eyes. These two were a piece of work for sure. Nothing like her at all. Tara wasn't here to win anyone's fortune. If any man did fall for their attempts to trap them, she hoped they had the wisdom to create a prenuptial agreement, so these women didn't end up taking them for every dime they had.

"You must be, Tara." Kelli walked over to her and extended a hand.

Tara debated whether to shake it or not. Deciding it would be rude to decline, Tara put her hand in Kelli's. "Hello, Kelli."

"I help coordinate events here at Beau Reve. I keep it running while the investors are away or while they play."

Kelli winked at her, and Tara blushed. Kelli was quite an attractive woman. Her hair was reminiscent of Marilyn Monroe, with the well-coiffed blonde curls enhancing the natural beauty of her face. Kelli truly was stunning.

"Come along now, dear. These two are pros now, but this is your first trip. Tell me, what do you think you'd like to do at Beau Reve?"

Tara fell into step with Kelli and tried to think of an answer that would make her flying here worthwhile. None really came to mind. Nothing exciting, really. "I'm on vacation. I don't have any expectations."

"Well, the sky is the limit here at Beau Reve. Handsome strangers need not apply. We've already got plenty of those." She winked at Tara.

"She said she was going to sit on the beach and read books." Sienna threw her two cents into the conversation.

See, catty. Tara had known it the moment they first started speaking. She was starting to wish she'd never left home. At least back there, she knew what she had. Here…. Well, if all of the people acted like this, she'd probably never leave her room. Tara fought the urge to sink into the ground and disappear.

Kelli eyed her seriously and shook her head. "Oh, honey. We're going to have to work on that shell of yours, I think. Maybe some speed dating later. That might work quite well."

"Speed dating?" Really? She fought the shivers that ran down her spine. Tara had never really tried that before. What was the point here, when she would only have two weeks to get to know a man better? Or was it more of a speed hook-up situation? That was probably more truthful.

"Yes, totally platonic. Just have a few drinks with some of our eligible bachelors. What could that hurt?"

Tara nibbled on her bottom lip. Could it hurt? It might be nice to actually talk to a man who didn't know her in real life. Maybe she could pretend to be someone else entirely, someone less boring than she actually was. At least she could tell Amelia that she tried something out. "I suppose that would be okay."

Madame Kelli beamed at her. "Good, good. Off to a great start then, I say. Beau Reve is a beautiful dream, my dear. Anything you dream—nothing more, nothing less."

"It is gorgeous here."

Tara was still looking at the scenery around her. Part of her wondered how well it held up to storms with all the hurricanes that had been hitting the shores lately. Stop that, she told herself. No need to start panicking about a fictional storm that would never come. That was the way her brain worked, though. Always ruining a good thing before it ever started. Most of her relationships were like that.

"A reward for living life well. Women who have good hearts, they need the most love in return, you know. I read your file. Caregiver to your brothers, head of the household. You've been a very good girl for a very long time, Tara. Now, let someone else take care of you, even if just for a little while."

Tara returned her smile and climbed into the limo. Thankfully, the other women hadn't heard what Kelli had just revealed about her. They'd have a field day. Tara wondered if they had a responsible bone in their body. How often had they come here again? Must be nice to just pick up and leave any time they wanted. She sighed and reminded herself that here was no different than anywhere else.

Tara made a resolution. It was time to live a little — just a teensy little. Not too much, because let's face it, she'd never be a candidate for a *Girls Gone Wild* video. She would only do the things she was comfortable with, even if it disappointed the people around her. Tara refused to let anyone make her decisions for her. She was too used to making them for herself, mostly because she'd had to for so long.

Drinks. Nothing serious. Tara took a deep breath and relaxed. Maybe she was going to be just fine here. It would be nice for someone else to take care of her for a little while. If she could actually let them. She'd start with the speed dating and go from there. Maybe she'd find herself living a little. If that were possible.

Who knows what might happen? Maybe she'd get a little wild for a change. Not that she'd tell Amelia. She wouldn't have to, though. Amelia would smell the sex on her even if she scrubbed every inch of her body. She was like a cat in heat on a good day. Amelia would definitely know.

"So, I have a question, Kelli." It was random, the one last thing that seemed to be holding her back from really trying to have a good time.

"Fire away, honey."

Tara tried not to look at the other women when she asked this. "I heard that Beau Reve is a place to have wild sexual encounters, but it seems a little like prostitution to me, considering that a benefactor paid for our vacations."

"Did she just call us hookers?" Sienna asked Rachel.

Rachel turned to her and shook her head. "Maybe you, but I'm pretty sure she wasn't talking about me."

"Like hell. You had more men than me last time. Sometimes three at a time, Rachel."

"Well, if the shoe fits!"

Sienna crossed her arms over her chest.

Kelli spit out the water she had just put in her mouth and patted Tara's arm. "Oh, honey. You're a peach. There is no prostitution. No expectations for women to put out anything they choose to keep for themselves."

"So, no strings?" Tara asked quietly.

"Nada. You want to have a sexy rendezvous with a handsome man or woman, that's up to you. There are no strings attached to your stay. None. Men are happy to pay for nothing at all if you get my drift. They enjoy just looking at a beautiful woman."

"Really?" Tara was having a hard time believing her. What man came here just to look at women? None she'd ever met. Of course, her world was filled with philandering jackasses out to squeeze a woman's ass just because she happened to walk near their tables, and they were supposed to just stand there and take it. That or lose their jobs. Tara had half a notion to report Lane, but it wouldn't take him long to retaliate. Maybe if she ever quit....

"Let me tell you the story of Nadia. She was a nurse who sat by the beds of dying patients for many years before she came here. Nadia met a wonderful man who not only swept her off her feet but allowed her to do more with her life. Nadia has created several foundations to help support nurses who provide end care for their patients and funding for patients that might not be able to go to hospice in a comfortable place. She is deliriously happy, and has four kids that she spoils rotten."

"So, she found a happily ever after here?" Why did that seem so impossible? Definitely really far from her own reality. Then again, would Tara be able to accept any man who tried to take care of her? Less than likely. She was far too independent for that and knew the worth behind working an honest day's work. How could she be with someone who didn't understand that?

"Yes. And she's not the first, and certainly not the last. Just be open to the possibility, and you won't be disappointed."

Hard to disappoint someone who has absolutely no expectations, but Tara didn't tell her that. She was here. Tara would enjoy being away from work and would try to keep an open mind. She took the glass of champagne that was offered her and kept her eyes trained to the beautiful tropical scenery in front of her. Blue skies, palm trees, and white billowy clouds—what more could a girl need?

When they pulled into the long drive leading to Beau Reve, Tara couldn't get over how large the resort was. She knew the beach wasn't far away from the resort, but it was hard to see from here. Beau Reve literally stretched as far as the eye could see in a series of different sized buildings starting with the larger hotel portion, down to the smaller bungalows. She wondered just how many people stayed there at one time.

They pulled up to the large white-faced building, and a doorman opened the door to let them out. The other women slid out quickly and headed straight into the building, almost as if they were racehorses at a race track. Eager for what, Tara really didn't know. She'd never been that eager for a man before. Good for them, though, she supposed. It must be nice to enjoy sex that much. She wouldn't really know. It had only been mediocre at best for the most part.

"Watch it, Rachel." Sienna shoved the blonde out of her way.

"Bitch, please!" Rachel shoved her harder, so hard that Sienna toppled to the ground.

Sienna straightened her tight dress as she stood and held her chin in the air as if she had any respect for herself. "Girl, I almost sprained my ankle."

"You should have worn your sandals then, Sienna." Rachel forgot their scuffle and offered her arm to Sienna. "Come on, you know there's plenty for both of us."

"Wow...." Train wrecks. They were definitely something.

"Unfortunately, some of the men actually enjoy their company," murmured Kelli.

"Well, they are beautiful." Tara shrugged her shoulders.

"Beauty is in the eye of the beholder." Kelli wrinkled her nose.

"I've never found that to be the case. Men rarely use their brains when women like that come around. They usually lead with their cocks," sighed Tara.

Kelli chuckled loudly. "Oh, you're a gem."

"If you say so." Tara grinned at her.

"Follow me, Tara. I'll get you all squared away." Kelli

gestured for her to follow her, which she did.

The main lobby of Beau Reve was decorated in rich blues and deep greens. The floor was white marble with different specks of blue that seemed to sparkle in the light. Large white marble posts stretched from the ceiling to the floor, and Tara wondered how much manpower it had taken just to get those in place. There was a large counter at the back that she assumed was the check-in desk because the other ladies were already chatting up the man behind it. Tara shook her head slowly.

"Yes, they are awfully needy today, it seems." Kelli clicked her tongue and shook her head.

"What do you mean?" Needy? More like clingy if you asked her.

"Come with me, my dear. I'll explain what it means to enjoy Beau Reve, and what it means to exploit it. Unfortunately, the billionaires never seem to spot the difference."

Wow. Tara couldn't believe how brutally honest Kelli could be, although if she were really honest, she would have said it to their face. Tara was about to ask her why she didn't say anything when Kelli put a hand up.

"Before you ask, yes. I told them that too. I've also told the men. No one seems to care as long as everyone is happy at the end of the day. I guess I should care about that more. But you, you're different." Kelli opened the door to her office.

"What do you mean?" What made her so different? She was maybe plainer than the others, but that was because she didn't paint her face like a two-dollar hooker. Tara nibbled her bottom lip to keep from giggling aloud.

"You need this more than they did." Kelli nodded back out to the lobby.

"I see." How did she not take offense to that? Kelli was basically calling her boring, right? Inexperienced? Dried out?

"No. You don't. You're like Nadia. You could use a good man. And not just sex, either."

"What if I like being independent?" She'd never really had a man in her life so far, and look how far she'd come. If only her brothers could understand that. They were constantly trying to push her into putting herself out there more.

"Oh honey, having a man in your life doesn't make you useless. These men could use a woman like you to set some of their priorities straight. Snag the right one, and you'll both be happier."

"And what if I don't want that?"

Because she didn't. She was not looking for a husband or a sugar daddy. Tara had been perfectly fine on her own. She had to admit the twenty-thousand-dollar check had been helpful though, even though she had felt guilty cashing it. If she hadn't, though, Amelia would have marched her ass into the bank to force her hand. She knew Amelia cared, but sometimes Tara thought she should worry about herself a little more.

"Then have fun at the very least. Go to a mixer. See if there's any promise here for you." Kelli took out some papers from her desk and handed them over to her. "This is an itinerary. It lists all the activities that you can do each day. Now, you mentioned sunbathing. Word of caution—the beach to the south is a nudist beach."

"Oh. Thanks." That would have been awkward. She assumed that not everyone here at Beau Reve was young and in shape. She wasn't sure she wanted to be naked in front of others, either. Actually, she was sure. It wasn't something on her bucket list, ever.

"Here is your ticket. You're on the first floor of the Bryant Building. Three buildings down from here. Your things will be delivered to your room. This is an all-inclusive vacation, my dear. Take advantage of our spa packages, restaurants, shopping. Go crazy. You deserve it."

"How do you know what I deserve?" Tara crossed her arms in front of her and tilted her head.

"Let's just say a little birdy told me. I'm a sucker for a sappy story. If only there were more responsible people like you in this world, I'd have more faith in humanity." Kelli smiled at her and let out a small breath. "Well, that's it. You're all squared away. My office is open if you ever need anything. The mixer is in the main hall tonight. Speed dating. Super fun for everyone."

"I'll give it a try." Speed dating, as far as she knew, was just a few minutes with each guy. Nothing serious at all. Tara could deal with that. "Thank you, Kelli."

Tara turned around and walked from the office. She'd head to her room and relax for the rest of the day. Then she would get ready for the evening and do her best not to look like a moron tonight.

Chapter 5

Tara took her time making her way to her building. She took in the world around her as she walked outside. The women seemed to outnumber the men from what she could see. For every man, there seemed to be three women, and from what she could tell, some of the women had no problem sharing.

"Well, at least they aren't money-hungry."

Not like the other two. She rolled her eyes as she thought about the two women who were so ridiculous. All they needed was a neon light flashing over their heads to let the men know they were an easy lay. Tara giggled at the image. What would the sign say over her head? Dried up? Old maid? Prude? Probably something closer to wears a chastity belt.

She nibbled her bottom lip and sighed. "This is going to be a long two weeks."

From the corner of her eye, she saw a small cabana was occupied. The sheets were blowing in the breeze, letting anyone see what was happening inside. Was that woman...? Tara blushed. Yep. Definitely naked, and riding the man beneath her like a bucking bronco.

"Oh my!"

Tara picked up the pace, suddenly ready to be inside her room to run scalding water over her eyeballs. The man the woman was doing wasn't all that attractive. It was probably his money she was after. Tara was fairly sure that Sienna and Rachel would still want more than money, though. Of course, if they found a less attractive man, perhaps he would actually marry one of them.

"Don't be crass, Tara," she chastised herself.

"Sorry?" A voice called from behind her.

Tara turned around and saw another woman standing behind her. "Sorry. I was talking to myself."

"Nasty habit," the woman teased her. She was a little older than Tara, maybe in her early thirties. "I've been accused of that myself from time to time."

"Thank goodness. I promise I'm not crazy." Tara held up a hand.

"Just don't answer yourself. Then people really lose their shit. I'm Abby."

"Tara." She breathed a sigh of relief. Her first impression of Abby was that she was down to earth, more like Tara. Especially considering the conservative way she was dressed.

"First time?" Abby asked her.

"Is it really that obvious?"

"A little. Don't worry, not everyone spends their time doing that." Abby nodded back to the cabana. "Some of us actually hold out a little longer."

"That's good to know. I was starting to wonder if I'd walked into a different universe altogether."

"Beau Reve can certainly seem like that. There are quite a few risqué things going on here, none of which you have to partake in — unless, of course, you want to. No one will judge you either way."

"I guess I should stop judging everyone else, then," mumbled Tara.

"It happens. Where you staying?" Abby asked her.

"Bryant."

"That's a quiet place. More conservative and private. You'll like it. I'm in the next building over. Gregory."

"Is Gregory...?"

"Quiet?" Abby smiled at her curiosity.

"Yes." Tara blushed.

"Sometimes. Other times…. Well, it's a good thing the walls are soundproofed." Abby winked at her.

"Oh." Tara giggled. Abby reminded her a lot of Amelia.

"And speaking of which, here's my stop. It was nice to meet you, Tara. Maybe I'll see you around."

"Yeah. Maybe. Have fun."

"You too, Tara. Fun is around every corner — you just have to turn it." Abby nodded to her before entering her building.

Well, at least Abby had managed to distract her. She had definitely needed it.

Walking to the next building, Tara found her room and pushed the key card in the slot. The lights turned green, granting her access to the room. She was actually surprised it had turned green the first try. Most hotel key cards took a few times before the lock actually recognized the damn thing. "Thank goodness."

As she entered the room, she was surprised to see how much space she actually had. This wasn't just a hotel room. It was more like a standard resort suite one might find on an expensive vacation. The living room was almost as large as the one she had back home. There was a small kitchenette, which made sense because most of the time, she'd be eating out somewhere on the resort. Really, the kitchenette was unnecessary.

Tara made her way into the master bedroom and smiled. Fit for a queen. There was even a large walk-in closet, which she didn't understand. Did people live in these rooms? She found a few hooks on the ceiling, which she found curious. What were those used for? Hanging plants? Or...? Tara blushed. Bondage, right? She opened one of the drawers inside the closet and found that her assumption wasn't that far off. There were several straps and cuffs of different sizes inside it.

"Well, they sure think of everything."

Tara chuckled. Not that she would be using them any time soon. Nevertheless, she pulled one out to smell it. Smelled clean to her, which meant they probably sanitized it after each use. Tara shivered in spite of herself as she put it back in the drawer.

Walking out of the closet, she discovered the large bathroom off to the left. It had a round garden tub that was to die for. Tara could really stretch out in a bubble bath in that one. Not like the tub back home, where she had to bend her legs to make them fit. Her tub was from the twentieth century and definitely needed an upgrade. At least it worked, though. Unlike the dishwasher that still needed to be replaced. One thing at a time. Besides, it wasn't like her fingers were broken. She was perfectly capable of handwashing dishes.

Tara looked just past the tub and found a glass tiled shower that was massive, with enough room for at least four people. That's probably why it was so huge. Shower orgy? There were a few large metal rings that reminded her of towel holders. She was pretty sure that they weren't used for that, but even still, she couldn't conjure an actual purpose. To hang on to while taking a shower? She let her mind go a little further and blushed.

"Oh...that's what they're for."

Grip bars for shower sex. She shook her head and

sighed. Was she going to be forced to think about sex during her entire stay here? No wonder women didn't hold out long. There were fantasies carved into every inch of its construction. Now her fantasy, that would be a library with a warm crackling fire. If she found a library like that here, it would probably have a faux fur rug meant for...not reading on.

She sighed and took a deep breath. "Two weeks, Tara. You can make it."

As she left the bathroom, she saw the king-sized bed had more than enough room for three people, obviously more than enough for her. Tara leapt in the air and plunged down on it, surprised by how comfortable it was. After spending close to eighteen hours with Sienna and Rachel, Tara needed a little respite. She wasn't sure how they still had voices, seeing as how they had talked pretty much the entire flight. Tara had tried to tune them out, but they were too loud. Their excitement had apparently been too much to contain. At one point, Tara had fallen asleep, but laying down on the soft bed was quickly draining her.

After sleeping most of her morning away, Tara ordered room service. The spread that was brought to her was delicious, making her wonder what else she might find at the restaurants on the island. At least her stomach would be satisfied. The rest of her.... Well, that was still up in the air.

Tara spent the rest of the afternoon by the side of her

private pool. She couldn't believe the luxury here at Beau Reve. On the first floor, each room had a small patio area that led to a private pool. Walls were separating the outdoor areas, making her feel like she had her own private backyard that looked out onto the beach behind her. Whoever had designed the resort had put a lot of thought into what each room should have. She couldn't help wondering if all the buildings were just like this, or had she been upgraded?

When she was done soaking up the rays, Tara went inside to dress for the speed dating. What should she wear? She didn't want to appear too easy, yet at the same point in time, she wasn't a schoolmarm. In fact, most of her clothes were low cut and fit her pretty tight. She was just more comfortable that way. It probably didn't help that some of her clothes were Amelia's cast-offs. "Hmm...what to wear what to wear."

Tara looked through her clothes and decided that her small red dress would be just fine. The small skirt showed off her legs, which was why Tara had made sure that they were as smooth as they could possibly be. While she wasn't out to find someone to jump into bed with, she had promised Amelia she would at least look at her prospects.

She looked in the mirror and shook her head. Her brown hair was a mess, but she had time to salvage it. Tara spent the next half hour creating an updo that showed off her neck. Why she didn't know. She wasn't really looking to attract anyone, right? Even so, she didn't want to look out of place either. She applied enough eyeliner to make her brown eyes pop, then some lipstick that didn't clash with her red dress. When she had completed her beauty rituals, she felt ready to face the evening.

Pulling out the map, she looked up the location for the speed dating mixer. After she found it, Tara made her way to the main hall. When she entered the room, she was surprised to find that the room was packed. She only found that odd because so far, she hadn't really heard anyone out and about. At first, she thought that meant that the rest of her building was empty, but then again, maybe the walls were soundproof, which was entirely possible considering Beau Reve was well known for its sexual proclivities. She'd been reading up on some of the possible activities here with the other materials that had been sent in the third package, which had arrived the day after she made her reservations. There seemed to be a place for every fetish one could imagine.

And then there were people like her, who had no fetish at all. Plain Jane's? Or was that considered vanilla if her sex-life consisted of nothing out of the ordinary? Dried up vanilla was probably a better term. She couldn't actually remember the last time she had slept with someone. Her experiences could actually be counted with her two hands, not even in the double digits. Pathetic, right?

Shaking off her thoughts, Tara decided it would be best if she didn't think too hard. Her brain had a way of keeping her stuck in the same old rut. If she were going to give this an honest shot, she had to be willing to do the unthinkable. Stepping up to the first free table, Tara waited for the speed dating to begin. Thankfully, she didn't have long to wait.

"Evening. I'm Tim." Tim was probably in his mid to late forties. He was an attractive man, but not really her type. Tara really wasn't into mustaches. Beards were okay, but mustaches by themselves just were a turn off for her. Too bad too. He actually seemed nice enough at first impression.

She took the hand he offered and smiled politely. "Tara."

"What brings you to Beau Reve?" His eyes seemed to be looking her up and down well before those words left his mouth.

Tara fought the urge to shiver. "I needed a vacation. You?"

"Same. And to blow off some steam."

By the way Tim looked at her; he thought about doing a lot more than that. He wasn't as good as she first thought. Clearly, he was here to find someone to spend his night with. Tara fought the urge to shiver in disgust. Maybe she shouldn't have made herself up quite so well tonight. This was already more uncomfortable than she cared to admit. They stood there quietly for at least a minute until the first bell rang. Thank goodness. She didn't want to stand around next to Tim longer than she had to.

Hopefully, she wouldn't feel as awkward with the next man. If he looked at her like a piece of meat too, Tara just might resign herself to staying inside her room for the next two weeks. This was already turning into her worst nightmare. It was bad enough that she had to deal with that same exact behavior at the bar. But there, she had to put up with it. Here, she could just walk away.

"Hi. I'm Todd."

"Tara." She took his hand and smiled as before. He was younger than Tim. Blond hair, blue eyes. Attractive too, but something about him turned her off right away, and she couldn't seem to put her finger on it.

This went on for another hour. One man traded for the next, and Tara was constantly reminded that she was not as willing a participant as some of the other ladies in the room. They were having a lot more fun than she was, probably even making plans for future hookups, but not Tara. She was feeling more uncomfortable by the minute.

When the next billionaire entered her table, it was all she could do to offer a smile. "I'm Tara."

"Ryan. Tell me, are you as bored as I am?" Ryan nodded to the room around them.

Tara looked down with guilt. "Does it show that badly?"

"Yes. It could only be clearer if you wrote it with a magic marker." His smile told her he was teasing her.

"I don't mean to be ungrateful. I'm just not sure this is

the place for me."

Tara looked away and gestured helplessly to the crowd around them. She was definitely not cut out for this. If the ground could swallow her whole right now, she would be forever thankful for that, especially considering the entertainment that was making itself known across the bar. Apparently, some of the couples were already pairing up and making quite a display of themselves.

"New here?" His voice brought her back to the present. The distraction was almost a relief.

"Yes. I almost didn't come." She straightened her skirt over her legs.

"Well, I'm glad you did."

At his words, Tara looked up at him and really looked at him. Unlike the others, Ryan was dressed in a simple cotton T-shirt and denim jeans. He was maybe late thirties tops. His blond hair was short and spiked. He was the first person who had approached her with nothing to prove.

"Thank you, I think." The bell rang, and Tara let out a disappointed sigh. It was the first time she had actually meant it that night. "It was nice to meet you."

"Would you like to skip out with me?" He gave her a bright smile, and she had to admit it was hard to say no.

"I'm not sure...." Tara certainly didn't want him to have the wrong idea. If she left with him, she was not going to sleep with him. He would probably assume she wanted more than she was actually willing to give.

"You have to eat sometime, right? Just a bite to eat? I know I'm starving." His gentle voice coaxed her.

He was right. She was hungry, and while they had been plying them all with beverages, there was no food in sight right now. Tara wondered if they were trying to get the women drunk, but surely that couldn't have been their motivation. No one was forcing the drinks down their throats. Tara had only been nursing one drink, knowing that if she drank too much, she was liable to get too chatty and voice her opinions about the world around her.

Should she go with him? He was actually the first man here who had cared about anything besides looking her up and down like a lamb for the slaughter. In fact, he barely seemed to notice her. "You know what? Yes. I'd love to get some food."

"Great. There's a nice grill near the beach if you care to take a small stroll."

"Sounds delightful."

Tara followed him out of the room and tried not to feel weird about the many eyes that seemed to be trained on them as they left. If this was the way Beau Reve worked, like some kind of auction for rich men, Tara would spend the majority of her time in her room. That was not something she would ever be interested in. Maybe money made them feel overconfident. Maybe they were actually overcompensating for something. She wasn't sure. For now, she'd just take some comfort in a nice stroll with a handsome man.

Chapter 6

"Don't let them get to you. This particular mixer seems to bring the idiots out in full force," he leaned over to whisper to her as they left the room.

"Thanks." She shook her head at him. What exactly did he mean by that? Was she one of the idiots? Hadn't he come to the mixer for the exact same thing? Had he just gotten tired of the way the women were looking at him? Actually, now that she thought about it, she hadn't seen him in the room before he slid into the seat across from her. Tara was pretty sure she would have noticed him.

"Not you. You're quite lovely, but you're not like that room of people." His blue eyes seemed to look into hers as if searching her very soul. Tara was slightly unnerved by them. Like the ocean before a storm, they spelled trouble. For her, at least. She could fall into them if she wasn't careful.

"How do you know that?"

She smirked at him and almost crossed her arms. She'd save that for later. Amelia often told her that both together was a scary combination, which was probably why she was still single. That, and her resting bitch face that seemed to cover her face most of the time, a technique she had needed to perfect while raising two teenage boys. Sometimes she wished she could have just been their sister and not their mother during their most turbulent years.

"Because you're a lot like me." He smiled softly at her, and Tara felt like he was actually peering through a window of her soul if that were possible.

Tara had to stop herself from giggling nervously. She deflected with her sarcasm, as usual. "So, some billionaire paid your way to a mystery vacation too?"

"No. I'm a billionaire too, but I made my money the hard way. I earned it. Those guys in there, not many of them know what it's like to do an honest day's work."

"Oh? What was the last thing you did at work? I waited tables, and then I washed crap off the bathroom wall." Tara challenged him to top that one. In reality, he probably couldn't. "And I do mean crap."

"I haven't done that in forever, but I did spend my time in those trenches. Ever hear of Damon's Pub?"

"Yes, there's one in every major city. Why?" The pub was a very popular sports bar that had started out when one tiny restaurant was made into a sports bar several years ago. She wasn't sure of the complete history, but it was a pretty popular place. Always busy and sometimes hard to get into on a Friday night.

"That's my pub. I opened the first one eight years ago using a startup loan from a bank."

"So, in eight years, you became a billionaire?" Tara shook her head in disbelief. How was that even possible? That kind of money would take her several lifetimes to earn. Definitely out of her realm of possibilities.

"When I'd made my first million, I invested in another business as a silent partner. I've been repeating that process ever since." Ryan gave her a cocky smile, but somehow his confidence didn't bother her.

"You're right. You're not like those men. But are you looking for the same thing they are?" Tara couldn't seem to keep the words from leaving her mouth. She didn't want him to think she was asking because she was interested. Tara did not want to lead him on. The chance of him getting an easy lay from her was almost non-existent. Almost.

"Am I looking for a little bit of fun? Of course. I'm breathing, right? And the women here are beautiful, but I'm not looking for someone who's goal is to shackle me. There are quite a few money grabbing women here. I'm steering clear of those."

"Good for you. I met a couple of ladies earlier today that seemed to think their cash cow might be here. Kind of sad, if you ask me. I've never looked for the easy way out. I never will. I'd like to be able to look at myself in the mirror every day." Plus, there was the fact that her parents had ingrained in her the need to be a responsible functioning adult that contributed something to society. Be the change you want to see, her mother always told her. The problem with that was Tara rarely ever saw anyone else change. It got old being the one to bend so often, but that was simply reality. Nothing ever changed.

"You're a breath of fresh air, Tara. Ah, here we are." Ryan gestured to an outdoor restaurant and helped find them a free table. It was a small picnic table with an oversized umbrella to protect them from the sun, which was just starting to set.

Pity that she hadn't gotten to spend more time in the sun today, but there would always be tomorrow. She slid down onto the bench of the table and put her hands in her lap, unsure what to do in this particular situation. Why did she always have to be so damned awkward around handsome men?

A waiter brought two menus to the table. "May I get you something to drink?"

"Water for me," Tara answered him. She'd start with that at least. Maybe she'd get something else when they ordered food, but Tara worked at enough bars to learn that she should always have a water handy to help counteract the alcohol. It helped her keep her wits about her a little better.

"Whatever's on tap, please," Ryan asked him.

"Right away."

Tara sat there in silence, trying to figure out what she was hungry for. There were so many things to choose from that she didn't know where to start. She looked up at Ryan helplessly. "Any suggestions?"

Of course, the waiter picked that moment to return to the table. "Your drinks. Do you know what you'd like to order?"

Ryan saw her dilemma. "How about a sampler platter? That way, you can try a little of everything."

"That sounds good. Can I get a margarita too?" She couldn't resist. Maybe it would help her find sleep easier tonight, especially considering how much she had slept this morning. Maybe after that, she'd find another fruity beverage, something with mango or passion fruit.

"Coming right up." The waiter took the menus and left the table.

As she looked around them, she wondered why no one else was at the grill. In fact, besides the waiter, no one else seemed to be in sight. "Where is everyone?"

"It's night time. Unless you're at one of the events, for the most part, you're indoors. Alone or not so alone." He grinned at her.

"You're enjoying my discomfort." Tara shook her head at him.

"Ah, you're just an easy target," he teased her.

Why did he have to be so handsome and likable? See, if Tara had known she was going to meet someone like Ryan, she might have been a little more open-minded about Beau Reve. Could she see herself in his capable arms? She found it a little unnerving how easy the answer came to her. Yes — hell, yes. Handsome, successful, not afraid of a little hard work, Ryan seemed to be the kind of man that would have attracted her outside this fantasy island. Of course, there he would be out of her league. Here, he was almost attainable, but only because he was intrigued by her. Wait until he got to know her better. He'd go to the next pair of willing arms as soon as he realized she was not going to be an easy lay.

"Right. I haven't been easy, ever." She gave him a half-smile.

"I don't mind, Tara. I like a challenge." He slid his hand over hers, and Tara felt a tingle of excitement run up her arm.

She shook her head at him. He was sure turning up the charm. It was only partially working, for her warning bells were already going off. "So, tell me what it's like to be a billionaire, Ryan."

"Not much different than it was to have nothing, to be honest. People expect money to suddenly make you fulfilled. Sometimes it's more trouble than it's worth."

"Are you lonely?" She didn't know why that question came out of her mouth. It was too late to pull the words back, though.

"Sometimes. I don't find myself short on companions, but none I like enough to keep around. And you, Tara? Are you lonely?"

Tara looked out at the horizon and sighed. "All the time, actually."

"That's unfortunate. Maybe it's time to do something about that?"

Ryan's eyes met hers, and she smiled.

"Nice try, Ryan. You'll need to find another angle." She shook her head at him, and when his blue eyes sparkled at her, she knew she hadn't completely misread the humor in the situation.

Their food arrived, and Tara went about trying everything, hoping it would distract her from that handsome smile. He was right. It was delicious. She finished the first margarita, and another one soon replaced it. Before long, the alcohol was going to her head, even though she was drinking a fair amount of water.

Ryan seemed to notice this. "Would you care to take a walk? You look like you could use the air."

"Well, that's silly. We're already outside, Ryan. How much fresher can the air get?" She shook her head at him and tried to bite off a giggle. Oh, dear lord. Here came the happy drunk who was not able to keep her mouth shut.

"Just trust me, Tara. I promise you'll enjoy the walk."

"Fine. A walk. But then I should really call it a night. Long flight and all." Tara was worried about how much trouble she could get into, especially when half of her was more than willing. Tara could not afford to open that door, though.

"Gentleman's honor." Ryan crossed his hand over his heart and held up his right hand. He stood up and offered his arm, which surprised Tara.

Walking next to Ryan in the moonlight ended up being the best part of her night. They walked along the beach with the moon's rays echoing around them. It was hauntingly beautiful. The warm air blowing on her face was restoring a little clarity to her mind. When he stopped and turned to face her, she looked up at him in confusion.

"What are you doing, Ryan?"

"Just enjoying the view." He ran a hand along the curve of her chin and smiled softly at her. When his mouth came down to hers, Tara knew she could back away, but she was curious. His lips were gentle and sweet on hers, soft like velvet. He deepened the kiss and brought her closer to him. Tara slid closer into his embrace, just enjoying the simplicity of the moment. Ryan was the first to break the kiss.

"That was...." Tara was at a loss for words. Every inch of her body was now aware of his presence. What would it be like to give in to her curiosity? It wasn't a stretch to see herself in his arms, but Tara had been clear that she wasn't here for that, right? How could she just turn around and change her mind? She wasn't a fickle woman.

"Nice doesn't seem to sum it up." Ryan pulled her close, but this time simply offered his arms. "I'd love to see what else might be between us, Tara, but I won't be making a move on you tonight. If you want to see what tomorrow brings, you're welcome to find me. I'm at the Drake house, one of the condos further down the beach."

"Aren't you just looking for a good time?" She tilted her head and tried to discern what Ryan wanted.

"Not a good time, Tara. A very good time. I'd be lying if I told you I wasn't imagining you naked in my bed and pretty much anywhere else I can take you. I may have worked hard to get where I am, but I am a flesh and blood man. I also understand if that's not what you're looking for."

"I'll think about it, Ryan. Right now, I'd like to go back to my room. But I'd like to do one last thing."

"Oh?"

Tara put her hand on his face and tilted her head up for another kiss. When his tongue delved into her mouth, Tara felt as if electricity were racing through her body. She'd kissed plenty of men—usually, that was the only base she'd let them get to—but if any of them had kissed her as thoroughly as Ryan did right now, she probably wouldn't be standing here at Beau Reve with a handsome stranger. She'd have already found someone special in the outside world by now for sure. When the kiss broke, Tara had trouble collecting her thoughts. He was certainly talented.

He rested his chin on the top of her head. "Let me walk you to your room, Tara."

She looked up at him suspiciously, but his charming smile was hard to deny. "Okay."

He walked her back to her room and, like the gentleman he claimed to be, stopped at her door. "Good night, Tara."

"Good night, Ryan."

"One for the road?" He asked her softly.

"Sure." She was breathless in anticipation.

His mouth came down to hers, and Tara sighed against him. He definitely ranked high on her list of best kissers. Maybe even at the top. She would have to kiss him a little more to know for sure, but not tonight. She did not want to lead him on, for while her body was definitely attracted to him, she was not going to fall into his arms that easily. He had his work cut out for him if that was his endgame.

Ryan broke the kiss and stroked her cheek softly. "Until next time, Tara."

"Maybe I'll see you around." She sure hoped so. Her toes were curling inward at the thought of another kiss, but she pushed those thoughts aside. "I might go to the beach tomorrow."

"Which one?" His eyebrows rose curiously.

"Not the nudist one, if that's what you were thinking." She held up a finger at him.

"Guilty." He grinned at her.

"Thought so. Do all men have the same one-track

mind?" she asked him curiously.

He held a finger up to check his pulse. "As long as we're living and breathing."

Tara slapped him on his arm, playfully. Ryan wrapped his arms around her and brought his mouth so it was close to hers. She shivered in his arms, anticipating the touch of his lips, a touch that didn't come right away.

"I'm all about the seduction, though, Tara. When you finally come into my arms, you'll never want to leave."

His mouth finally came down to hers, and his tongue slid into her mouth. Tara shivered against him as his hands massaged the small of her back. When he let her go, Tara missed the heat of his body.

"Until tomorrow, Tara."

Chapter 7

He left her there to find her way inside alone. She closed the door behind her. Tara touched her lips and smiled in spite of herself. "What are you going to do, Tara?"

Now she was even talking to herself. It was a nasty habit, really. At least she only did it when no one was watching her. Otherwise, they'd probably think she'd lost her mind or something. Honestly, she already felt like she'd gone around the bend, letting some handsome stranger kiss her. At least Amelia would be proud of her, up until the point where she found out Tara had gone to her room alone. Ah, well, she still had two weeks to work up the courage to explore her options.

Beau Reve was turning into more of an adventure than she'd thought it would be. Her plan had been to keep to herself most of the time. The problem with that was that it was what Tara always did. She had one good friend, and that was about it. Sure, the girls at the bar were social with her, but they were young and carefree. They had very little in common. And while Tara was not an old maid, she often felt like she was. She'd already raised two boys into men who attempted to adult from time to time. That was more than most people her age could say.

Tara sighed. Wasn't it getting old, doing the same old thing? The results were always the same. Boredom. Malcontent. Sometimes, depression. Amelia was right. Maybe it was time to kick up her heels and enjoy life for a little while. What could it hurt? Had she known that they wouldn't all be skeevy jerks, she might have been a little more open-minded. That didn't mean she'd sleep with Ryan, but she also wasn't completely ruling it out.

Her eyes were certainly open now, and she was happy to explore her options. Not that she'd tell Amelia. That girl would just be filled with I told you so's. Tara could never tell her about it. Not if she wanted to keep her dignity intact. Amelia would want all the details, and Tara wasn't sure she could tell her anything without blushing from head to toe. As it stood, nothing had really happened yet, although Ryan was plotting her seduction.

Seduction? She shivered at the thought. Had she ever been seduced? Not really, or if so, not very well. Tara was actually looking forward to that prospect. How would he go about doing that? Step by aching step? What if it took too long? Would he get bored and move on to the next available woman? Tara sure hoped not. She would hate to miss out on the experience.

She nibbled on her lip as she thought about the strong arms that he had wrapped around her. His lips were definitely kissable. What a waste it would be if she didn't explore him further. Tara would have to make sure that he knew she was interested enough to keep him playing along.

Maybe he liked women who played hard to get. Then again, if she was that hard to get, she would never have let him kiss her the way he just had. She shivered, just thinking about it as she walked into the bedroom. As she changed into her sleepwear, she saw that her desire for him was quite visible in the way her nipples perked up. Had he noticed? She was torn between hoping he had missed it and wanting him to notice. Tara was a mixed-up bag of feelings tonight for sure.

When she climbed under the sheets, she sighed against them. All she had to do now was fall asleep, which was hard to do, considering there were parts of her body that were throbbing. She touched her mouth again. If he was a good kisser, chances were he was a fantastic lover. Shivering slightly, she tried to close her eyes and think about the sleep that was so far out of reach.

"Good luck with that, Tara," she told herself wryly. All she had to do was get him out of her mind, but the more she lay there, the more she wondered what it would be like to have his strong arms wrapped around her.

Tara rolled over and punched one of the pillows. She wasn't that easy, was she? Honestly, just a few kisses, and all she could think about was jumping on top of the poor man. Well, rich man, and a very interested one. She sighed. "Nope. You are not going after him, Tara. You're just going to have to count sheep."

Sheep...right. Trying to conjure anything but his smiling face was going to be difficult right now. Too bad she'd left her toys at home. Sometimes a good orgasm helped her fall asleep when she was overtired.

"Ah, well," Tara sighed.

She took out her book, hoping it would lull her to sleep. As she turned the pages, she realized that none of the words had even registered. She went back and reread them, forcing herself to focus. Once she got back into the story, it got a little easier. Tara read until her eyelids started to droop. She fell asleep with it on her chest.

That night when Tara slept, she didn't get the peace she hoped she would find. Instead, she dreamt of the handsome billionaire. At first, it was a soft and gentle dream of a man who was only interested in romancing her, which was a nice change. Then the dream turned into something else altogether. His arms and mouth were everywhere at once, and when Tara woke up, she was extremely aroused. Her fingers curled up in frustration.

"Well, that didn't work."

Tara had tried to make herself dream about anything but Ryan. It was ironic that she'd come here prepared to swear off any kind of interaction with the horny men on the island, and here she was hornier than she'd ever been.

"Get it together, girl."

Tara yawned and stretched in her bed, wondering what the day would actually bring. Apparently, her mind had sinful things planned if Tara would reach out and take the bait that was dangling right in front of her. How far was she going to let him push her before she gave in to him? The chase was thrilling, but Tara would not be able to hold out forever.

She remembered their kiss last night. Soft and sweet, yet there had been an undercurrent of desire she hadn't felt in quite some time. Was it possible to give in to it without having regrets later? Did sleeping with someone she barely knew make her a whore? And what did it matter if it did? No one here knew her. It was only her own mind she would have to worry about.

Tara pushed her legs over the edge of the bed and stood up. Time to shake her thoughts from her head. This morning she was beach bound. She walked to the bathroom and turned on the shower.

When she stepped under the hot steamy spray, her mind immediately turned to things best left alone. Her dream revolved in her mind, and she had trouble focusing. By the time she stepped out of the shower, she was even more hot and bothered than she had been moments earlier.

"Damn it, Tara. Pull yourself together."

She found the black suit they had sent and quickly threw it on. Tara wrapped one of her sunbathing skirts around herself and found the little bag she'd brought to take with her to the beach. Packing a beach towel from the bathroom, she added her sunblock and her book. She didn't bother to bring anything to eat or drink, because the beach was sure to have some kind of refreshment area.

Tara double-checked that she had everything she needed, including the key to her room, then she was ready to go. With her sunglasses on top of her head, she was ready to conquer the beach and anything or anyone that came with it. Even if it meant spending the day in solitary.

The beach wasn't that hard to find. Thankfully, she remembered not to head to the south. Nudist beaches might be for some people, but Tara just couldn't imagine laying there with all her parts exposed to the rest of the world. She wasn't ashamed of her body; she just didn't think it was something she needed to put out there. There would be no snatching and grabbing—no way. Well, not unless Ryan convinced her otherwise. Then maybe she might consider it.

As Tara made her way down the small wooden walkway, she was happy to find there were several loungers available. She chose one a little further down on the beach, in hopes that it would discourage others from interrupting her peace and quiet. She spread her towel over the lounger and sat down.

She was only laying there for a few minutes when a shadow blocked her sun. Tara turned to find Rachel and Sienna, and fought the urge to roll her eyes. "Good morning, ladies."

"Good morning. Tara, right?" Sienna asked her.

"Yes. Sienna and Rachel?" she asked for clarification. Not that she really needed it. These two were definitely not forgettable at all. She was pretty sure they would be the punchline to many jokes for the next two years between Amelia and herself. Amelia may love sex more than most people, but she was not like these two. If she had been, she would have snagged a husband a long time ago. She'd had plenty of opportunities.

"Yep. Mind if we join you?" Rachel asked her with a voice so bubbly that it irritated the hell out of Tara. She would prefer nails on a chalkboard at this point.

"Not at all." Liar, she told herself. Far be it from her to be rude, though. It was simply not in Tara's nature. She'd just have stick it out and hope that they didn't do anything that made her lose her mind.

"Good." Sienna gestured to a worker nearby. "We'd like some drinks. Two mimosas. What would you like, Tara?"

"Water would be great." It was a little early in the morning to be drinking, but then again, these two looked like they might be pretty used to day drinking. Tara forced herself to bite her tongue. Rocking the boat was certainly not going to get her anywhere.

"So, what did you do yesterday?" Sienna probed.

"Not much. Just laid around mostly. You?" Tara didn't really care what they had done, but she was trying to be polite. Nor did she feel the need to tell them about the handsome stranger who had kissed her so thoroughly.

"Tried out a few options." Sienna winked at her. "And then met up with Rachel for a swing party."

Did she dare ask what a swing party was? Two thoughts popped in her head—multiple partners or actual swings. Was that even a thing, though? She knew they made sex swings, but imagining a few of them in the same room seemed almost scandalous. Either way, she was sure it ended up with both of them getting laid—if not once, multiple times.

"Find what you're looking for?"

"Not yet," answered Rachel. "But there's still time. Maybe we'll see a few while we're here."

Yes, please find some horny man to walk off with. Tara would even help if it meant they left faster. Hell, she'd wave a flag that said "Easy chicks" with an arrow pointing at them if it would help. Create a landing strip and signal to them like an air traffic controller. She smiled and tried to keep herself from giggling. Oh, someday her thoughts were going to get her in trouble.

Tara sat there for the next three hours, listening to the women talk about all their sexual escapades at Beau Reve, and tried not to look for a stick to shove into her ears. Why hadn't she brought her headphones? At least she could have kept her eyes closed and pretended not to see them. They were clearly drunk, and it wasn't even noon yet. Tara just didn't get it.

When Sienna squealed unexpectedly, Tara almost jumped out of her chair. She turned to see what the problem was and saw Ryan walking closer to them.

"Ryan!" Sienna jumped from the lounger and launched herself at him.

Tara was surprised that she knew him, but then again, not so surprised. He was devilishly handsome and rich, something that would have drawn her to him immediately. Tara watched Sienna kiss him hard on the lips. He didn't seem to be turning her down, not at first, but when he saw Tara watching them, he set the redhead away from him.

"Hello to you too, Sienna. Still haven't found your man?" He asked her teasingly.

"Well, you keep saying no." She pouted at him and held her chest up higher. Tara was afraid the woman's breasts would spring out of her suit if she angled them any closer.

"Just as well—there are plenty of men here this week. Maybe you'll snag one yet."

When Sienna tangled her arms around his, Ryan grimaced slightly. Tara took pity on the poor man and rose from her lounger. She kissed him on the cheek and stroked his face. "You're late."

Confusion fluttered across his face at first, then he realized what she was doing. His mouth came down to hers and planted a slow sensual kiss on her lips. "I missed you, Tara."

If looks could kill, Tara would have imploded on sight. She fought the urge to chuckle at the redhead's glare. Tara couldn't help it—she was definitely enjoying this.

"It's only been a few hours." Tara wrinkled her nose at him.

"Absence makes the heart grow fonder," he returned as his hand slid across her ass.

"I wasn't aware your heart was in your pants." She giggled when Sienna walked off in a huff. Thankful she had left, now Tara could really start to have some fun. Tara couldn't wait to see what the day would bring.

Ryan leaned over and kissed her again. He held her close enough for him to whisper in her ear, "Thank you."

"Any time," she beamed up at him before smacking him on the ass with her hand.

"Watch it, you," he warned her. "You're playing with fire."

"We have an audience." No, they didn't, but she wasn't going to tell him that.

"I see. Care to take a walk?" He offered his hand to her.

"Sure. Will my stuff be okay here?"

"Definitely," he assured her.

The day was just about to get interesting. Wherever it led, Tara was willing to follow its path. It was well past time for her to take a chance on something new. Besides, in the end, she could leave it here, but she'd still have the memories to last her a lifetime. Wasn't that worth something?

Chapter 8

Before she could second guess herself, Tara took his hand. She smiled when he brought it to his mouth. His silky lips tickled her flesh, and she fought the urge to shiver. She couldn't let him see how much he affected her. Showing her hand too soon was never a good idea.

"So...."

"So," he answered as they walked down the beach. "Have any big plans today?"

"Not really. Just a little fun in the sun, I guess. I've never been to anywhere this beautiful before."

As they walked, Tara saw that they were moving down the beach to where the loungers seemed to disappear completely. Was this a stretch of private beach? Hopefully, he wasn't leading her to the south beach. Tara looked up at the sky and tried to determine where the sun was behind her. The bright light almost blinded her. That's what she got for not trusting him.

As they continued to make their way down the beach, Tara took in the simple beauty around her. Everywhere she looked, the sand seemed to glitter from the sun's rays. The bright aqua waters looked almost hand-painted, the colors were so vibrant. The water looked almost crystal clear. The last time she'd been to a beach was in Carlsbad, California, where the sand was covered in debris carried in from the ocean. Either the beach was better maintained, or the waters were just that much cleaner here. Beau Reve was a paradise in more ways than one, she supposed.

"Ever surf?" Ryan broke through the silence that had fallen between them.

"Surf?" She looked up at him as if he'd lost his mind. "Uhm, that would be a big fat...nope. I've never even been in the ocean."

He whistled. "Wow, you are a little sheltered."

"Hey!" She shoved against him. "I went to the beach, but the waters were so filthy I chickened out."

"No time like the present." Ryan scooped her up in his arms and started to carry her toward the water. When she started to shriek, he positioned her, so she was slung over his back, almost like a bag of potatoes.

"Ryan! Put me down!"

She started to pound on his back with her hands, squealing like a little girl as he carried her out to roaring waves. When he finally let her down, she slid down his body. She felt his heat against her and shivered. What was he trying to do to her?

"Cold?" His blue eyes searched hers.

Tara was pretty sure he already knew the answer. Her heart was beating so loud in her ears; she was sure he could hear it. Not to mention that her arousal was already standing out against her bikini top. That was entirely his fault for the way he'd slid her down his body.

"*No...,*" she whispered right before his mouth came down to hers. Tara sighed against him as his tongue delved into her mouth. Closing her eyes, she let the moment take her. His hands wrapped in her hair and held her closer as their tongues dueled for control.

If it had not been for the large wave crashing into them, the kiss could have gone on for eternity. They both toppled under the force of the waves, and Tara found herself slipping underwater. She was a little afraid because she'd never been knocked over by anything like that before. Tara saw the white bubbles of air rippling around her and fought her way through the wave. Trying not to panic, she relaxed her body and waited for the water to recede slightly before pushing up to the surface. She sputtered slightly when she finally broke free.

"You okay, Tara?" Ryan called over to her from a few feet away. The force of the water had separated them.

"Yeah, I think so."

Except now she was down one piece of clothing, a fact

that Ryan had already noticed as he made his way closer to her. Tara crossed her arms over her chest and tried to balance in the water as the waves continued to crest. Unfortunately, she could only cover so much. She was pretty sure he could still see more than she'd exposed to any man in the past two years.

When he pulled her against him and kissed her again, Tara released her breasts and slid her arms around his neck. She felt her nipples press into his skin, and she shivered against him. The friction of that tiny little movement made her want so much more than he was giving her right now.

Sensing another wave coming their way, Ryan lifted her against him. She clung to him and felt her breasts press hard against his chest as he carried her to the beach. He laid her down on the sand and stroked her face with his hand.

"The ocean can't compare to your beauty, Tara." His words were believable. Tara realized he was much better at this than she had thought. Or was she just that easy to convince?

She saw him staring at her state of arousal, and she started to blush. Tara tried to hide her bare chest again, but Ryan took her hands in his. He held them over her head as he trailed kisses down her face. He released her hands, but Tara didn't move them. She was transfixed in the moment, desire starting to tingle through her body. His mouth came down on hers as his fingers moved over her breasts gently. When a finger flicked against her nipple, she flinched slightly. Wrapping her arms around his head, she pulled him down closer to her.

He continued to kiss her as his fingers teased her more. "I think you like that."

Tara sighed against his mouth when he kissed her some more. She'd be a fool not to like the way his hands and lips made her feel. Or half dead. She'd have to have one foot in the grave to not notice him. He was nothing short of fantastic, and she would do anything just to have one night with him. Even if it meant pushing herself to her own personal limit.

Much to her disappointment, Ryan broke the kiss and pulled away from her. "One moment."

Tara watched him walk back to the water, and saw him snatch the top of her bikini from one of the waves. He strode back to her, and she tried to reach for it.

"Ah-ah. Allow me?"

Tara felt her eyebrow rise. She stood up and turned around. "Fine."

Ryan wrapped his arms around her waist and pulled her tight against his body, so close that she could feel the erection that was growing hard between them. His fingers caressed her stomach as he slid the scrap of material around her. When his hands cupped her breasts, his mouth whispered at her earlobe, "I could have you right here, Tara."

She clenched her stomach and felt a jolt race through

her body. "What are you waiting for?"

Tara felt him jerk against her slightly. Ryan flicked his thumb over her nipple before covering her breasts with the bikini top. He tried the strings firmly around her and kissed her shoulders before turning her around.

"We've only just begun, Tara."

His mouth ran small, delectable kisses up and down the flesh of her back. Tara's body was priming itself for him, whether she wanted it to or not. Every inch of her was filled with heightened awareness. His hands caressed her stomach as his mouth seared a path downward.

She nibbled on her bottom lip. He could have had her right then and there. Tara wouldn't have complained in the least. Every inch of her craved his touch. It was unfair to want someone this badly, so easily. Her brain was no longer thinking of consequences. Every nerve ending was firing signals of desire that coursed through her body like molten lava.

Ryan pulled her against him and nuzzled the curve of her neck. When he breathed his hot breath on her skin, she shivered. His lips took her in, licking and biting the most erogenous zone on her body for just a little while before he pulled away from her. He turned her around in his arms and kissed her softly on the cheek.

"You look so disappointed," he teased her.

Tara looked away. "You're not playing fair, Ryan."

"Who says I'm playing?" His mouth covered hers

again, and he pulled her closer to him.

Every inch of her body relaxed into him. He appeased her with his kiss, a kiss that took her breath away. By the time he finished, Tara had almost forgotten her name. She leaned her head against his shoulder and sighed. "You're very good at that."

Ryan's chest shook with a slight rumble as he chuckled at her words. "You're a breath of fresh air."

"Glad someone thinks so." Tara sighed. For most people, Tara was stale, undesirable. Could he really find her refreshing? Attractive?

"Fools, every last one of them," he said before he kissed her again.

This time, his hands roamed up and down her back, coming to rest on her ass, where they massaged against her lightly.

"So, what did you think of the ocean?" He asked her quietly when he broke the kiss.

"It's a little too frisky if you ask me." She smiled up at him.

"Apparently. My kind of waters." He winked at her.

"What else do you have in mind for today?" Tara asked him. She was definitely curious as to where this day might actually lead them.

"Maybe some lunch?" he suggested.

"Good. I'm starving." Had she even eaten breakfast? Tara actually couldn't remember anything past the last ten minutes. He made it easy for her to forget herself.

"Me too."

By the flash of his eyes, it was clear that Ryan was not talking about food. Tara fought the urge to dig further because while she was pretty sure he could have had his way with her, the way he was dragging it out made her want it that much more. She was pretty sure he knew that too.

"Let's go eat." He winked at her and reached for her hand.

Tara took it, knowing she'd let him lead her to the fiery pits of hell if it meant she'd eventually wind up in his arms. The day could only get better from here. If she was lucky, it was about to get really good.

Chapter 9

They made their way up the beach, and Tara made it a point to ignore the jealous eyes that followed her. It wasn't her fault that Ryan was not looking for a money grabbing attention seeker. She was sure some men would fall for it, but not this one. It was a good thing she wasn't really after the end game like they were. Tara was so used to being alone, she wasn't even sure what she'd do with an actual relationship.

As she grabbed her things, she heard Sienna whisper to Rachel, *"What does he see in her?"*

Tara had wondered that very thing herself, but still, it wasn't very nice of her to be so catty. Tara pretended she hadn't heard them, even though they weren't being all that quiet about it.

If Ryan noticed, he never said anything. That was probably for the best. She didn't need a knight in shining armor to deal with a jealous harpy. They were a dime a dozen at the bar. Girlfriends were always particular when they went out with their boyfriends. It was like they had to pee all over them to mark their territory or something. The funny thing was, half the time their men already had one foot out the door.

She had done a lot of crowd watching over the years as she tried to figure out how the world turned. Always on the outside looking in, that was how she'd spent most of her life. Tara was simply used to missing out on life. Today, though, she felt like she was living, and that was a first for her. She felt more carefree than she ever had, and she was looking forward to seeing which direction it led her.

"Let's get a cabana." Ryan pointed to one of the bright blue tents that offered privacy. "We can have one of the cabana attendants bring us food."

"Sounds good to me." Although the seclusion made her slightly nervous, Tara shook off the unease. She was pretty sure he would not push her further than she was willing to go. He could have had her back at the beach, and he had barely done a thing.

They made their way over to the cabana and slid inside it. Tara watched him signal to one of the attendants. She sure couldn't fault them for their service here. She looked around the cabana and saw a few chairs and a long padded bench that sort of reminded her of a massage table. Considering there was a basket of lotions right by it, Tara had a good idea of what the table was used for.

"What can I get you?" The attendant asked them.

"Tara?"

"A fruity drink, please," Tara answered. "And some kind of food."

"Do you like seafood?" Ryan asked her.

"Love it."

"Seafood platter and a fruit platter, too, I think."

"Do you want the usual?" The attendant asked him.

"Sounds good," Ryan answered him.

The usual? Tara fought the urge to ask him how often he came to Beau Reve. Billionaires could come here any time they pleased, it looked like. Just how active was he? She couldn't help thinking how nice it would be to just pick up and go any time she pleased.

"So, what do you like to do in your free time, Tara?" Ryan asked her. He sat down in one of the chairs.

"Sleep." She grinned at him. "I work almost twelve-hour shifts seven days a week."

"Why do you work so hard?" he asked her.

"I know, all work and no play make me seem pretty boring. But I'm helping pay off my brother's college loans. He doesn't know that, though."

"What do you mean?"

"I lied to him. I told him my parents had left enough to help him with it." She sighed. "When I was twenty, my parents were killed in a head-on collision. Clay was fourteen, and Eric was only twelve. I was twenty, barely old enough to take charge, but somehow I managed."

"I can't even imagine."

"You'd think I miss them less each year. I always seem to miss them more." Tara gave him a half-smile. This wasn't something she really wanted to be talking about right now. It was morbid and depressing. Tara did not want to ruin the moment between them.

"They must have been amazing people." His voice was soft and sweet, completely unexpected.

"Why do you say that?"

"The fact that they raised such a responsible daughter who knows the value of keeping a family together despite the odds." Ryan seemed impressed.

"It's family. It's what we do." She gave him a big smile and waved away the sadness in the air. "What about your family?"

"I never knew my father. He died when I was a baby. My mother raised me by herself."

"No siblings?"

"Nope. Just me. I was enough of a handful for her." He winked at her.

"I doubt that." Tara waved his words away, even though a part of her could understand what his mother worried about. How many women had he known in his lifetime? All ready to throw themselves at him, no doubt. Considering how easily he had seduced her, he had plenty of practice. Tara was as reluctant as they came.

"Sure, you say that now. If you only knew." He wrinkled his nose at her. "I was quite precocious."

"Was?" She teased him.

"Hey, everything gets better with age."

"Says you." Tara rolled her eyes. Nothing was getting better for her. Just the same old thing day in and day out. She was starting to feel rather crusty about all of it.

"How old are you?" He asked her curiously.

"Twenty-five. Almost twenty-six. You?"

"Thirty-two. Older than the hills."

"Like hell." Tara shook her head at him. Was he fishing for compliments? "I like older men."

"Good. I'd hate for that to be a deal-breaker." He grinned at her.

"Deal? Did we have a deal?" Tara's voice was innocent. She knew what he was talking about, but she wasn't about to let him know that. Playing hard to get only seemed to push him further. Tara wondered just how far she could push it.

At that moment, the attendant knocked on the cabana. Ryan answered him. "Come in."

"Here are your drinks and food." He entered with another attendant, who was carrying trays of food. They set it on the small tables and bowed before leaving.

"Wow, that's a lot of food." Tara couldn't believe how much food came on their platters. It could feed a small army. Everything in Beau Reve was done to a larger scale than other places. Tara started to feel like they were being wasteful.

"I guess we'll just have to work up enough of an appetite." Tara shook her head. He was definitely incorrigible. She reached over to take a shrimp but ran into his hand. She withdrew her hand and smiled at him.

"Allow me."

He dipped the shrimp into the cocktail sauce and held it up for her to try. Tara took a bite and managed to get sauce on his hand. Her tongue snaked out to lick it off, and she reveled in the way he sucked in his breath. He had not been expecting her to do that.

"That was delicious."

"Care for another?" he asked her.

"I would." Tara nibbled on her bottom lip as she waited for him to hold another one up for her. This time she got sauce on her face, which she thought he had orchestrated.

"Turnabout is fair play. Let me help you with that."

Ryan licked the sauce from her face, and at the last minute, latched onto her lips. Tara wrapped her arms around his neck and pulled him closer. Their tongues dueled for control. In the end, he mastered hers, and Tara was not sorry.

When he pulled away, she was almost breathless. "That was nice."

"Nice? I need to up my game then." His eyes twinkled

merrily.

Tara wrinkled her nose. "I look forward to it."

For the next hour, they took turns feeding each other in the most erotic way. Tara was hot and bothered, for while she wanted more, he kept her at arm's length, pushing forward slightly, yet retracting from the moment without following through. He was definitely having way too much fun with her seduction. And while she was crazy for his touch, she was not going to complain in the least. Tara was definitely enjoying every minute of it.

"You seem tense. Let me help." He led her to the table. "Lay down, Tara."

"I'm not sure that's a good idea." She was on her second drink, and they had been fully loaded with strong alcohol. Alcohol always seemed to raise her rate of arousal. If he continued to touch her, she would lose her mind. As it stood, she was already wet.

"Why not?" His lips turned into a delicious smile, proving he knew without her even telling him. "Relax, Tara. I promise I won't take advantage. Just want to work out some of those knots."

Work out knots? He'd be working out a lot more if he pushed it too far. She'd be liable to jump him. Would he push her away? God, she hoped not. The idea of taking him deep inside her made her quiver in anticipation.

"You can even leave your clothes on," he said innocently as he watched every one of her reactions.

"You mean what little clothes I'm wearing?" Tara put a hand over her mouth and blushed furiously. She lay down on the table before she could say another word that would get her into trouble. Tara was nervous and was having trouble breathing. "I might need another drink for courage."

"Breathe, Tara. Relax. I'm not going to eat you."

"Only because you ate too much shrimp," she mumbled against her arm.

"I heard that." His voice was amused, at least. He poured oil on her skin and started to smooth it in. The oil seemed to warm her skin; the more he worked it in. Maybe it was the peppermint inside it. If he used too much, she was going to smell like a candy cane for three days. She didn't mind, though. The warmth it created was actually quite delicious.

"That's nice," she murmured. It was too. She couldn't remember the last time she'd had a massage. Two years ago, maybe? A gift from her brothers, although it wasn't nearly as nice as the one she was getting right now. Every inch of her was tingling as he woke up nerve endings that had been sleeping for far too long.

"Turn over, Tara."

Tara didn't want to do that. She was well aware of the way her nipples were standing out right now. She was past aroused. She ached for him, but she couldn't admit it. He'd already pushed her away once today. He wasn't toying with her to be cruel; Tara knew that. Try telling that to her body, which had a mind of its own right now. It craved so much more than his touch.

Tara turned over slowly and kept her eyes closed. She didn't want to see the affirmation in his eyes. He said nothing, just continued to work the oil over her body. When he was done, Tara ached for more of his touch.

Opening her eyes, she found he was just inches away from her face. Tara took a chance and reached up to kiss him. When his lips came down to hers, his fingers strummed over her nipples slowly, and Tara felt a quake in the pit of her stomach. She wanted him more than she thought possible, but he pulled away from her.

Tara sighed and sat up. "You, sir, are a tease."

"Yes, but you'll thank me later. It's getting late, Tara. I'd like to take you snorkeling tomorrow if you're up for it."

She favored him with a smile. "I've always wanted to try that."

"Good. Come to my place in the morning when you're ready to go. I've already chartered a boat for the day." He grinned at her.

"Well, you were awfully sure of yourself."

"No, just hopeful." His eyes twinkled. "Now, let's get you home."

Pity. She could stay here longer, staring into those beautiful eyes. Stormy ocean, with their wicked little gleam.

Ryan was more than she had ever bargained for. She only hoped she wouldn't be a disappointment when he finally conquered her shores. Would he stake his claim or pass her up for someone else? She couldn't help but think how disappointed he would be when it was all over. Would he consider his time wasted?

He brought her hand to his mouth and kissed it tenderly. "You look deep in thought. Care to share?"

"It's nothing worth sharing." She waved his concern off. "Boring, actually."

"I don't think there's a boring bone in your body, Tara."

"You haven't seen them yet. They're definitely there." She grinned as she pointed to her collar bone. "Like that one, right there."

Ryan leaned over and kissed it before nibbling it slightly. Her breath caught in her throat as he sucked it slowly. "Yep, definitely not boring."

"What about this one?" Tara pointed to her elbow.

"Hmmm…tricky."

Ryan lifted her arm into the air. He ran his hand across her chest, tweaking her nipple as he kissed her elbow softly. Tara whimpered slightly as he continued to lick and kiss it while running little circles around her areola. When he released her arm, she let it fall slowly to her side.

"That one seems intriguing too."

"You're a wicked man, Ryan."

"Yes, I am."

His mouth crushed hers with a kiss that robbed her of her sanity. When he finally broke it, Tara was trembling. He rubbed her bottom lip with his finger, and she fought the urge to nibble it. "What are you doing to me, Ryan?"

"Pushing the limit just a little, Tara. You'll thank me for it later. Let's get you home before I change my mind."

Would it be so wrong for him to do that? Especially since she wanted him badly. Surely he knew that by now. Anyone could see it. It wasn't just her face that was flushed. Every inch of her tingled from head to toe, and it wasn't just the peppermint oil causing it. She shivered as they left the cabana. She wasn't ready to face reality yet, but he was giving her no choice.

Chapter 10

The next morning, Tara was nervous as she slid out of bed and went to the mirror. Looking into it, she shook her head at herself. "Lighten up, Tara. What's the worst that can happen?"

Let's see — pregnancy, sexually transmitted diseases, and the worst of all, a broken heart.

Tara made a fist and shook it at herself. "Stop that! Damn it."

This was the reason why she couldn't find someone. She was too wound up and set in her ways. She might as well be a virgin — her well was certainly dry. Or it had been before she'd met Ryan. Now she was almost flooded, but he had yet to take a drink. She'd have to do something about that soon. All this seduction was going to be the end of her. The more he teased her, the harder it was for her to get any sleep. It was a cruel punishment indeed, considering she wasn't likely to go looking for any other man on the island, whereas there was nothing stopping him from taking his desire out on another willing woman. If he did, she didn't want to know about it. It would crush the illusion he was weaving around her.

If only it were easy to be so careful and forget about the repercussions. Tara had watched the others at the mixer the other night. The women were happily engaging with the men as if there was nothing to it, but for Tara, it was way more complicated. Up until now, she'd been disappointed with the male population. The thing was, with Ryan, she had no expectations, except for maybe he finished what he started. If he didn't, maybe she should find someone else to fulfill her. That could certainly be arranged.

"Give him one more chance, Tara." She tried to convince herself that it wasn't quite time to give up yet. There was ecstasy at the end of this journey, Tara was sure of it. Even if he was playing with fire right now.

Tara looked through her clothes and decided to put on her bikini under a blue sundress. She almost had a little pep to her step, knowing that she would be spending her day with Ryan. She'd never gone snorkeling before. This was definitely going to be a day to remember. She only wished she had an underwater camera to take pictures of all the tropical fish.

Who knew what else today would bring? First things first, though. Time to find Ryan. Tara looked at her map and found the Drake house. If she took a walk along the beach, she'd run into it eventually. She didn't mind a walk.

Putting on her sandals, Tara let herself out her back door and crossed around the private pool to the back area where the path led to the beach. As she walked along the beach, she saw that several people were already out and about. Some were sunning themselves on the white sand. Every once in a while, she got a peek of some questionable activities, but the small gazebos were covered with billowing material that made it harder to see if people were having sex out in public so early in the morning. Tara wondered what it would be like to be so free that it didn't matter who else was around her. What she wouldn't give to feel that freedom.

By the time Tara reached the Drake house, she was starting to rethink her plan. When she'd started the morning, she was ready to do whatever it took to make sure he finished what he started. Now she was in her head again. Tara clenched her fists and took a deep breath. Nothing would happen if she didn't want it to, she was pretty sure of that, but still, she was taking a risk. Amelia would tell her to go for it. Tara, she was just so used to staying the course, to doing the same thing she always did. Why did she have to be such a chicken shit? Time to live, Tara. Grow a pair, so to speak. Or at least borrow a pair. She bet Ryan's were nicely formed. Maybe she could borrow his for a little while.

Tara walked up the path leading her to the large bungalow house and stood just outside the sliding glass door. Should she go around to the front? Tara took a deep breath and knocked on the glass. She bit the bottom of her lip as she waited for Ryan to answer.

What if he was out? Or he could still be asleep. Maybe she should have called him. Wouldn't the operator have his number? She was about to turn away when she saw Ryan peek his head around the corner. When he saw her standing outside, he smiled and put up a hand to indicate he would be right there.

Did he have someone else there with him? Could she blame him if he did? Ryan knew what he was getting when he went to Beau Reve. *Please don't let it be Sienna.* Tara would never be able to look at him the same if she was there. That woman was despicable. The worst cat in heat she'd ever met. She might be beautiful, but sometimes beauty was only skin deep.

She let out a slow breath, trying to calm the thoughts that were swirling inside her head. Relax. She was here, that was the first step. "Breathe, Tara."

Before she could second guess her thoughts, Ryan came out to greet her. "Sorry I took so long. I had to throw some clothes on."

"Oh?" Now she saw that he must have been in the shower. "How was the water?"

"Warm enough. Come on in, Tara." He waved her into

the bungalow, and Tara looked around. It looked pretty much like her room, except the proportions were on a bigger scale.

"I had food delivered. Would you care for some?"

Tara put a hand to her stomach and smiled. "That would be lovely."

The island, with its fresh air and sunlight, had given her quite an appetite. Maybe it was the delicious food. She hadn't eaten since the cabana last night. Her mind had been on other things, things that would take energy. Food was a good idea. She sat down at the small table and smiled at Ryan as he did the same. In the early morning light, Ryan was still devilishly handsome. Today he was wearing a white cotton shirt with a pair of swim trunks.

Ryan handed her the platter with the fresh fruit and Danishes. They looked delicious. She loaded up her plate and took a quick bite. "Thank you. I didn't realize how hungry I was."

Ryan's blue eyes met hers, and a sexy smile slid across his face. "If you keep talking like that, a guy's going to get ideas, Tara."

"Oh? What kind of ideas?" And would they involve him actually following through? She was up and down, inside out with her emotions this morning. The one that came through the most was her need for him to make the first move.

"That maybe it will be my lucky day." His eyes

roamed over her exposed flesh, and she almost shivered in anticipation.

"Who knows, Ryan. Maybe it will be—if you're interested." She sure hoped he was. It's all she seemed to dream about now.

Ryan chuckled and shook his head. "I'm human, you're attractive. I'd be a fool not to be. But your seduction requires a little finesse, Tara. I haven't put in nearly enough time yet."

"Oh?" Tara tried to hide her disappointment. She wasn't sure what she expected. To jump his bones first thing in the morning? Tara was sure the other men here would have no problem with that scenario at all. Honestly, would he really stop her if she pushed the issue? Could she?

"The best things come to those who wait."

"I see." How long was he planning on waiting?

Tara bit into a slice of melon, and some of its juices dripped down her chin. She licked the corner of her mouth and used a napkin to wipe the rest away.

Ryan's eyes were on her every movement. Tara suddenly felt a little braver. She remembered the way they had fed each other last night, simple, erotic foreplay that had been innocent, yet enticing at the same time. Was he remembering it too? She nibbled on her bottom lip and closed her eyes. Tara heard him suck in his breath before the shuffle of a chair.

His mouth came down to hers, and she smiled against

it. He wasn't so difficult after all—he just needed a clear invitation. Her arms reached up to stroke his hair when his tongue slipped into her mouth. Tara felt her heart jump in her chest when he scooped her up in his arms and carried her in the air. Where was he taking her? His bed? Dare to dream, Tara. At this point, he could take her on the kitchen floor, and she'd be happy.

When he pushed open the sliding glass floor and set her on her feet, she broke the kiss.

"Ready to go?" He asked her with a teasing smile.

"I thought you were...." Tara's frustration only seemed to grow.

"Kissing you? Yes, but now it's time to show you something new. This is a vacation, Tara. Time for you to see what one looks like." Ryan rubbed his thumb over her lip.

"Snorkeling, right?" Tara asked him.

"Don't look so disappointed, Tara. There will always be time for that later."

"I mean, I guess I just thought—"

"Don't worry, Tara. When I'm ready to take you, you'll know."

"Good. I don't like to be kept in the dark." Tara sighed in frustration.

"Come here, Tara."

Ryan took her hand and brought it to his lips. He slid his arms around her body and tilted her chin up to look deep in her eyes. His mouth met hers and devoured every inch of her lips. Tara felt the heat climb in her body, twice as fast as the night before. When his hands slid down her back and grabbed her ass, Tara murmured against him. His mouth trailed down the side of her face, to where her ears met her neck.

"You are ripe for the picking, Tara. But no matter how delectable you are, I'm not going to fuck you right now."

She shivered at his words. So crass, yet exciting at the same time. When his mouth returned to hers, she wrapped her arms around his neck and held him tight. She felt the tension leave her body, and when he backed away from her, she was happy to see the kiss had affected him more than he'd probably care to admit.

When she managed to get her breathing under control, Tara looked at his face. He was watching her carefully. "What?"

"Let's go before I change my mind." He grinned at her.

Tara was half tempted to push the limit, but the anticipation was building inside her. When he finally did make his move on her, she would fall into a puddle at his feet. She took his hand and wrinkled her nose. "Let's do it."

His eyebrow rose curiously. "Oh?"

"Snorkeling," she clarified.

He chuckled. "Yes, snorkeling."

Chapter 11

They made their way to a dock on the other side of the island. As they walked down the wooden ramp, Tara started to feel a little foolish as she stopped right before the boat. She was afraid she would miss the edge and fall into the water.

Ryan saw her dilemma. He climbed onto the boat and gave her his hand. "I got you."

Tara grabbed his hands and closed one eye as she climbed over to the boat. He caught her easily in his arms and helped her sit down. "Thank you."

"Any time. Getting out is much worse."

"You're not helping." She wrinkled her nose at him.

"Ever been on a boat before, Tara?"

"A long time ago." Almost a lifetime ago, the one time her parents had taken them all on a boating trip for the weekend. Those had been some of the best memories. Too bad there weren't more like those.

"Well, this is a cabin cruiser. We'll dive off the back end there. If you need a restroom, there's one down in the cabin. I've had them stock the fridge with plenty of food for the day."

"There's one in here? Where?" Tara was perplexed.

"Let me give you the tour." Ryan gestured to the stairs leading down into the cabin below.

Tara followed him below and was surprised at how much room was down there. There was an L-shaped couch with a table that folded down to the floor. Across from there was a flat-screen television—why she had no idea. A small kitchen area was next to the entertainment space, with a medium-sized refrigerator and a microwave just above it.

"This is the head." Ryan pointed to a sliding door.

"Head?" Tara giggled slightly until he rolled the door open. "Oh, right. The bathroom. What a strange word."

"I never really thought of it." He grinned at her. "This is the bedroom."

Bedroom? She nibbled on her lip. Would they use that later? She sure hoped so. All she had to do was a role reversal. Maybe seduce him to the point where he couldn't push her away?

"What's going on in that head of yours, Tara?" He saw right through her.

"Nothing," she mumbled. "Should we get this show on the road?"

"You're cute when you're deflecting." He pulled her close to him and kissed her softly. His mouth trailed kisses back to her ear. "We'll see where the day takes us."

Shivers ran up and down her spine. She was looking forward to that. "I'm open for anything."

"Good. Up we go. No need to tempt fate, Tara."

She followed him upstairs and fought the urge to jump on his back and drag him back to the bed. *Patience, Tara.* When he finally did follow through, it would be more than worth it. The waiting was torture. She'd never been so aroused by the mere presence of a man. He was electrifying.

Ryan took the captain's seat, and Tara sank down into one of the benches across from him. She turned around to watch the waves under the boat as they slid through them with ease. At one point, she thought she saw a dolphin, but it ducked under the water before she could point it out.

When the boat stopped, Tara was unsure how far away they were from Beau Reve. Not that it mattered. Out here, she had him all to herself. She was anxious to see what would happen next.

"This is one of the best spots to see the reef." Ryan took off his shirt and slung it over the chair.

Tara pulled her dress over her head and smiled up at him. "I'm ready."

"Follow me." He walked out to the diving area. Reaching into one of the compartments, he pulled out two pairs of flippers and two snorkels. "Make sure your mask is tight, Tara."

Tara pulled the mask over her head and tightened the straps to make a seal around her face. Then she bent over and attached the fins to her feet. When she was about to put the snorkel in her mouth, Ryan showed her how to use it.

She followed him into the water and kept close to his side. For the next few hours, they explored the different areas of the reef. She had never seen such color in her life. To see tropical fish in their own habitat was breathtaking.

When they finally rose above the surface, Tara pulled the snorkeling mask from her face. "That was amazing."

"Let's take a break." Ryan gestured to the cabin cruiser and started to swim back to it.

As he helped her onto the diving platform, she couldn't help wondering how many women had fallen for his charm. Did it matter, really? She wasn't naïve. Tara knew this was only going to be another fling for him. He would probably move onto the next woman easily. Tara didn't think she'd get out quite as lucky as him, but that was the nature of the beast. One slice of heaven would be better than nothing at all. A memory to last the rest of her life, maybe one that would encourage her to be more open to a relationship with someone else in the future.

They sat there for a few moments, gathering their breath. She looked over at him and smiled. "Now what?"

"You're awfully anxious, Tara. What would you like to happen next?"

"I'm open to suggestions." She was completely open to them. If he didn't make a move soon, she would start giving him a few.

"I see. Let's have lunch first. You're going to need energy for what I have planned."

Oh? She wondered what was next. Excitement started to race through her. She took a chance and reached over to kiss him on the mouth. Ryan slid his hands behind her back and pulled her close for a long kiss that turned up her thermostat to boiling. When he pulled away from her, she saw he was just as affected by it.

"Food, woman." He stood up and offered her his hand.

"Pity," she grumbled.

Ryan chuckled but did not comment. He led her downstairs to the galley and pulled out some of the food from inside—sandwiches, a veggie platter, and fruit. "Hope you're hungry."

"Starving." She eyed the fresh fruit, which, of course, made her think of yesterday. Wicked man. Tara had a feeling he had that put there purposefully. As she nibbled on her food, she saw him watching her every movement. "What?"

He reached over and wiped his finger across her lips. "Some mustard."

Tara pulled his hand to her face and licked the mustard off before sucking his finger into her mouth. Ryan shoved the food to the other side of the table and folded one half of it.

"Come here, Tara."

She nibbled on her bottom lip. "I thought you were hungry."

"Oh, I am, but not for food."

Her heart leapt in her chest as she allowed herself to be pulled into his arms. His mouth slid over hers gently, and she sighed against him, praying he was going to follow through this time.

When the kiss turned up in intensity, he slid his hand to her back. His fingers worked her ties loose on her bikini, and Tara sucked her breath into her chest.

"So beautiful, Tara," he whispered into her ear. His mouth began to trace a path down her neck, and she shivered in reflex. When his lips touched the base of her neck, Tara moaned softly. It had been far too long for her.

His lips continued to travel down, and when his mouth connected with her breast, Tara arched her back and pulled him closer by pressing his head with her hands. He growled against her chest and lifted his mouth just slightly. "You make it hard to resist you, Tara."

"Then don't."

His mouth returned to her breast, and his tongue snaked over her nipple. Tara whimpered against him. "You're ripe for the picking, Tara."

"Please," she whispered.

He lifted her in his arms and carried her to the bedroom,

where he lay her back against the bed. He sucked her nipple into his mouth, and she arched against him. "Do you like that, Tara?"

"*Yes.*" She definitely liked that. And when he nibbled lightly on it, she whimpered aloud.

He released her and came up to kiss her again. This time his lips moved with an intensity that made her feel like she would liquify beneath him. As he kissed her, his hand slid down to her legs, then found their way to where her legs came together. His movements taunted her slightly. Sliding her legs open, she craved his touch.

"You're almost there, Tara." He worked on the ties that held her bikini in place, and soon she was completely naked before him. "Exquisite," he murmured against her lips.

His hand slid down to her clit, and Tara arched against his hand. He moved his fingers against it, at first in a slow motion, and Tara felt her insides start to burn. With his mouth burning a path of fire on her aching nipples, his fingers worked their magic down below.

When she thought she could take no more, he slid a finger inside and used her moisture to lubricate her clit. The next time he moved over her, his fingers moved fast and hard, so fast she lost the ability to reason. Her insides bunched up, and she ached to feel the release behind it. She tried to fight it, to stop it from coming, but it was like a freight train—unstoppable. Even though he had only been working her over for a few minutes, Tara came hard against his hand.

"That's it, Tara. Let it all out." His mouth covered hers as he continued to work her over. She came again, and this time, Tara called out his name.

"Ryan!"

"Like music to my ears." He growled against her mouth before moving down to take in her left nipple. He sucked her hard into his mouth as his fingers continued to force another release.

This time when she finished, his tongue plunged into her mouth, mimicking the movements she wanted to feel deep inside her. Her heart raced as he kissed her so hard she thought she'd lose consciousness. Ryan had been so controlled, but now he was starting to look a little wild and dangerous, and she loved every moment of it.

He pulled away from her and took a staggering breath. "One moment, Tara."

He pulled his shorts down, and she could see his swollen erection. Reaching into a drawer under the bed, he pulled out a condom. Tara watched him slide it slowly over him, and she licked her lips.

His body seemed to shiver at her appreciation. Ryan smiled that sexy smile that could knock the moon from the sky. "You sure you're ready, Tara?"

"God, yes," she whispered. She was still admiring his cock. It was magnificent. She'd had enough experience to know Ryan was well-endowed. She couldn't help wonder what it would feel like to have him buried deep inside her.

He slid over her with the prowess of a panther. When he sank slowly into her, Tara shivered in anticipation. His movements were slow at first, driving her to the end of the line and shoving her over before she could even question it. As she quivered around him, he stiffened above her.

"If you keep that up, this may be over too soon," he teased her.

She clenched around him, and he growled before shoving hard into her. Her breath caught in her throat as he picked up the speed. Tara met him thrust for thrust until a wildfire broke out inside her. She bucked against him as another orgasm stole the very air she breathed. Ryan rode it out and found his own finish with a guttural groan.

He rolled off her and pulled her close to him. "That was definitely worth the wait."

She sighed against him. "Inspired."

"Why don't you rest up before we start round two?" he suggested.

"Oh?" Her mind was still hazy from round one.

Ryan moved away for a few moments. When he returned, he brought her a glass of something bubbly. "A toast to the sea."

"To the sea."

When she finished her drink, she snuggled against him and drifted off to sleep with the waves rocking her. Tara was having the most wonderful dream. Her body was being carried on a wave of ecstasy. She was dreaming of Ryan's handsome face and the way he took her breath away. Tara felt a warmth fill her as he took his fill of her body.

As she started to wake, she saw that her dream was, in fact, reality. Ryan was running his hands all over her body while his tongue ran small circles around her areola before sucking her nipple into his mouth. Her breath caught in her throat as she arched into him.

"Mmmmm..." she moaned softly. "What do you think you're doing?"

"It's not every day I wake up with a naked woman in my arms," he murmured against her breast.

"I see." Tara giggled but was cut off by his mouth as he covered hers. His tongue slipped inside, and she sucked it hard into her mouth. They dueled as his fingers slid down between her legs.

He drove her into a frenzy but stopped just before she could finish and withdrew his hand. When she calmed down, he worked her over again. He was a master of seduction, taking her so far, yet holding ecstasy just a little out of her reach.

Finally, Tara had enough and pushed him off her. She reached down to the basket and ripped open one of the condoms with her teeth.

"What are you doing, Tara?" He asked with a devilish tint to his eyes.

"Taking what I want, since you keep teasing me."

"I see."

"Lay back, Ryan," she ordered him.

He seemed to like her forceful tone, for he laid back, propped up by the pillows behind him. "Your pleasure is my own."

"Damn right it is." Tara reached for his cock and slid the condom over it very slowly. There was more she would have liked to do with it, but her need was far too great right now.

"Come here, Tara." He beckoned her closer.

Tara climbed over him and brought her face to his. His mouth covered hers, and he pulled her closer to him. Tara straddled his hips and sighed when he slid his dick into her. The heat of his cock was scalding even through the latex. She reveled in the delicious feel of it as he coaxed her body up and down along its length. She was tight around him, and she knew that had more to do with his size than her lack of experience.

"God, you feel so tight, Tara."

She moaned against him as his hands brought her hard down on top of him. She almost felt impaled by his cock, but she took every inch of him into her. She let her head fall back and rode on top of him. His hands covered her breasts and squeezed them hard as she rode him. Before she knew it, her juices were covering him.

"That's right, Tara. Let go, baby. I have you."

And he did. Over and over, he drove into her. Tara

had never been with someone with such stamina. When he finally found his own orgasm, Tara was dripping wet over him. She let herself fall against him and put her head on his shoulder. Ryan ran his hands up and down her back. His gentle touch made it easier to forgive herself for letting go so easily. For some reason, the walls that she kept up around her had come toppling down the moment she met him. Tara couldn't make sense of it. Maybe she wasn't supposed to. Flings were like that, right?

"That was amazing." Her words came out in an amazed whisper.

"That was just an appetizer," he promised her.

She sat up and looked at him. "Oh? It gets better than this? That's hard to believe."

"Anything is possible at Beau Reve. You have two weeks. More, I think, if you're interested."

"More?" Tara did not allow herself to think of what more could mean. It didn't exist in her world. She knew better.

"I can always buy more time," he offered.

Tara looked away from him. Suddenly she felt like a high paid prostitute. Next thing he'd do was offer her money. She climbed off him and tried to choose her words wisely. There was no need to make him feel bad. This was just the way his world worked. "This was a lovely day, Ryan. I'd like to head back to the island, though."

"Big plans?" he asked her.

"You never know," she answered, but refused to look at him.

"Let's head back then. Shall we?" He bent to retrieve her bikini. "You might want to get dressed before we get there. Not that anyone would mind seeing you naked."

"Right." Tara quickly cleaned herself up with a towel and then put her bikini back on. She slid her blue sundress back over her shoulders. She watched as Ryan put his swim trunks on. What a shame to hide such a beautiful body from the world.

Of course, if the other women saw how well-endowed he was, she'd have to fight them off with a stick. That was if she were still interested in pursuing more time with him. She sat back and looked out across the ocean as they made their way back to Beau Reve.

Chapter 12

When they made it to shore, Tara was still trying to decide what she would do. Her feelings were a little hurt; the more she thought about it. She knew she should have never come here. She was starting to feel cheap and needy. The combination almost made her sick to her stomach.

Clearly, Ryan was interested in only one thing—sex. He had spent a fair amount of time stringing her along, making her fall for a fantasy that he had woven around her far too easily. Tara had been a fool. He had managed to do in three days what took most men months. Maybe she should be thankful that he was showing his true colors.

Tara sighed. Could she blame him for being the way he was? He had been upfront with her this whole time. He was a living, breathing man who may not be completely consumed with sexual fantasies, but aware enough to want a woman who was hard to get. Sex was something that was probably second nature to him.

Most of the women and men who came here were here for that same thing. They were living out all of their sexual fantasies. Most were probably well satisfied. The problem was, Tara was not like the others. She was going to have a hard time compartmentalizing her emotions. Right now, she felt a little used, even though he had made sure she was well taken care of. Ryan was a considerate lover, making sure she had her fun before he allowed himself free reign. Tara couldn't complain about that. Really, she couldn't complain about anything. She had put herself in this position.

Ryan jumped off the boat and tied it to the dock. Then he reached down to offer his hand to her. Tara took it, only because she was afraid she'd miss the dock without it. When she was standing next to him, she pulled her hand free.

"Is something wrong, Tara?" he asked her.

"What do you mean?" She deflected. Of course, there was something wrong. One question, and he had ruined everything. If he had just never said it, then Tara would not be second-guessing everything. She would still be reliving each and every moment in her mind right now. Instead, she was tearing herself apart one piece at a time.

"You're awfully quiet." His eyes were trying to read her, but Tara's walls had come up again.

"Just tired. I guess a day of...sun, will do that to me."

Tara offered him a feeble smile. "I think I'm just going to go back to my room for the night."

"Pity. I was hoping you'd join me."

Tara sighed. "Not tonight, Ryan."

"Did I do something wrong, Tara?" He reached for her hand, and she let him take it. They started to walk back up the beach, but she refused to answer him. Ryan stopped in his tracks and put his arms on her shoulders. "You're upset with me."

"No...," she denied. She wasn't really all that upset at him. It was her own pride she was working through right now.

"Tara...." His eyebrows rose as he waited for her to answer him.

"You ruined the moment, Ryan," she blurted out before she could stop herself. Ruined, shattered, obliterated. All feasible descriptions.

"Don't hold yourself back, Tara. Let it out before it festers," he urged her.

"I'm starting to feel like a high-priced hooker." There, she said it.

"I'm sorry?" He looked confused.

"Well, after...well...you know...you offered me more. But what your more meant was another week here on the island. I'd be an all-expenses-paid prostitute." Her eyes met his, and anger started to swarm inside her.

"I didn't mean for you to take it that way, Tara." His

face was filled with regret.

"And yet, here we are." Tara was a proud woman, at least she usually was. Right now, she was a little disappointed in herself. "I tried to tell you I'm not like the others, and you just kept pushing it."

"I'm sorry if I hurt you." Ryan really did look sorry.

"It's fine. I did it to myself, really." She sighed and looked away from him. "Maybe it's just a sign."

"So, what does this mean, Tara?" Ryan asked her softly.

"I'm not sure yet." She didn't want to completely push him away because she'd actually enjoyed his company. The sex was out of this world, but could she continue this path and walk away the same woman? Or would it change her forever?

"I'm not here for more than this," he said regretfully. "I thought you knew that."

"I do." She did know it. Tara wasn't trying to make him want more than a fling either. She just didn't want the illusion to change. Maybe she just needed to keep it all in perspective.

"Were you having fun?" He asked her.

"I was. I am. I'd like to spend more time with you." It was true. She did want to spend time with him, whatever that meant.

"Good." Ryan leaned down and kissed her softly on the lips and whispered, "I've got a lot more seduction planned for you if you're still interested."

"Oh, I'm interested. As long as we both know that this ends next week." Tara was drawing a line. "No offering more, Ryan."

"As you wish, Tara." He grinned at her, and she saw the relief in his eyes. "Still going back to your room?"

Tara sighed. "For a little while. I'd like to refresh myself if you don't mind."

"Of course. We could go out to eat, check out some entertainment — or we could be the entertainment."

Tara wasn't exactly sure what he meant by his words, but she wasn't going to ask him right now. "Give me a few hours."

"You got it. I'll swing by your place at seven?"

"Sounds good."

"Do you want me to walk you back to your room?" he asked her.

"No, I'm a big girl, Ryan. I can take care of myself." At least she used to think that she could. Now, she wasn't entirely sure. He had blown up her conceptions of what she was capable of. Could she continue to sleep with him knowing it was the end of the line soon? Her brain told her to run as fast as her feet could carry her, all except the zone that was tied up in the desire he had stroked far too easily. Yes, she could, and she would.

"Stop second-guessing yourself," she told herself.

"Still talking to yourself, I see," a familiar voice teased her.

"Abby! You almost gave me a heart attack." Tara smiled at the woman.

"Well, don't go doing that." Abby wrinkled her nose at her. "Wait. Stop right there."

Tara stopped in her tracks. "What? Is there a spider on me?"

"Turn around." Abby waved her hand in a small circle.

"O...kay." Tara turned in a slow circle, wondering what in the world was up with Abby right now. "Something wrong?"

"Wrong? Not in the least. You're glowing. Did you get some?" Abby teased her.

"Some...sun? Why, yes...yes, I did. Thank you for noticing. I was out snorkeling. The salt has a way of restoring the skin," Tara tried to explain.

"Honey, I wrote the book on deflection. You, my girl, got laid. And pretty well by the blush on your face right now," Abby teased her.

Tara groaned. "Ughhh...really?"

"Yep. But then again, I paid close attention to how you looked before. You almost look relaxed."

"Well, I was until he opened his big mouth." Tara sighed.

"Oh, dear, what did he do?" Abby gestured to a few chairs right outside her building. "Come, sit."

"Okay, but only for a few minutes. I have two hours before Ryan comes to pick me up."

"Ryan Star?" Abby was visibly impressed.

"Star?" Was that his last name? Abby didn't remember him sharing that information with her.

"Owns the Damon's Pub franchise?"

"Oh, yes. That's him." Tara sighed.

"He's a catch. Very picky, that one."

"I'm sure he could have his pick of women." Tara waved her compliment off.

"Yes, and he does indulge from time to time. But lately, he's been a little detached."

"Uhm...how often do you come here?"

"Come here? Oh, dear girl, I live here now." Abby wrinkled her nose at her.

"Say what now?"

"Oh, Tara. You're too precious. Yes, I'm a year-round resident, being a contributing member, that is."

"How's that?" Tara was pretty confused at this point.

"Dear girl, I helped design it. Of course, I was several years younger then. A young heiress just getting out of a horrendous relationship." Abby watched her with a smile. "Cheating bastard. Don't worry, I took him for everything he had."

Tara was still having trouble connecting the dots. "So, Beau Reve was actually created by —"

"Rich women, Tara. Rich women who made rich men pay to treat women like queens. At first, they balked at the idea, but soon it became so popular that the men started to fill the coffers, so to speak."

"But those same men come here hoping to...."

"Get laid? Sure, they do, but you best believe they have to work for it. Every time they stay, they pay for at least eight women to come here." Abby smiled. "And some of them are better for it. Not all women who come here are looking for a paycheck. Some find love when they least expect it. Others.... Well, they just find the fun that's been missing in their lives. I daresay no one is ever the same."

Tara was fascinated by Abby's tale. "That's brilliant. Turning the tables on the men. I wish I could do that."

"What do you mean?" Abby asked her curiously.

"I work at a night club that seems to cater to the men to the extent that it's okay for them to grab our asses any time they want to." Tara crossed her arms over her chest and held her chin out.

"He doesn't throw them out?" Abby's eyebrow rose in annoyance.

"No. Just stands there and watches. I'd have a bouncer."

"Have you ever thought about calling the cops? That is assault, you know."

"I do know, but what good does that do but get us all fired?" Tara shook her head. "The system is stacked against us."

"It does seem that way sometimes." Abby looked thoughtful. "You never know when change will come your way, though."

"If it does, it's been a long time coming."

"So have a lot of things, I'm thinking. How was it?"

Tara blushed. She knew Abby was talking about her time with Ryan. "It was...magical at first."

"What happened?"

"He offered to buy me more time, so I could stay longer, and he could...."

"Have more sex with you? Come on, say it. Sex. It's not a bad word, you know. The very act is quite liberating."

"It was until it was framed in a way that makes it feel like prostitution."

"Did he make you feel like you had to have sex with him?"

"No."

"Did you want to have sex with him?"

Tara blushed. "Yes. Very much so."

"Do you still want to."

Tara sighed and shivered as she thought about the way he had made her feel. "Yes."

"Well, then live a little, I always say. As long as you stay grounded in a little bit of reality. Besides, I think he has taken quite a liking to you." Abby grinned at her.

"If you say so. Anyway, we're having dinner somewhere tonight, and then...we'll see."

"I shall hope the night concludes with you having mind-blowing sex." Abby winked at her. "What? There's nothing wrong with it."

"No, there's not. I'm just not as carefree about it."

"Understandable. If you stay here long enough, everything becomes second nature. But like I said. I live here." Abby winked at her. "Go get gussied up, dear. Make sure you take control over the situation, though. Give him what for and make him crave more, I always say."

Tara smiled at her. "You're a good listener, Abby. Thank you."

"Any time. Just don't tell everyone who I am. I've kept most of them guessing for quite some time. They're starting to think I'm a horny cougar."

"You're not that old, Abby."

"Fifty-five last Wednesday."

"Really?" Tara wouldn't have guessed that at all.

"Sex keeps one young, Tara. It's all those delicious endorphins."

"See you around, Abby."

Tara smiled at her before she stood up from the chair. As she returned to her room, she took in what Abby had told her. Two things stood out the most. Ryan was very picky in who he chose to sleep with, and sex was good for the soul. Okay, put those two things together, and she was convinced that sleeping with him wasn't going to break her into millions of pieces in the long run. She just had to make sure she managed her expectations. Sex, not love. Their time was limited, so Tara would just have to take what she could get. She'd carry it with her for the rest of her life.

Chapter 13

By the time Ryan came to retrieve her, Tara had showered and changed into one of the sundresses that she had brought with her. It was a simple red dress with a ruffle that ran along her collarbone and over her shoulders. She had her hair up in a simple French braid and had added a small red flower at the top of her braid. Tara could have tried a more dramatic effect with her makeup, but he'd already seen her naked—what did it matter what her face looked like? She went with a more natural look, the same thing she'd done every day since forever. In her mind, it was better that she felt comfortable in her own skin rather than impressing other people.

When the knock sounded on her door, Tara took a deep breath and tried to remind herself of everything Abby had told her about Ryan. He was not like the other men. He was picky, so if he had chosen to be with her, then she should trust his reasons. Like Tara, he wasn't looking for a relationship, so leaving it to a casual vacation fling should be easy. Should be. Tara was still working out a few of the bugs in her head, but most of her was on board with that.

Tara opened the door and smiled. "Hello, Ryan."

"You look lovely," he complimented her.

Tara reached up and kissed him softly. "So, do you."

Ryan pulled her closer and kissed her longer. Tara sighed against him, realizing that if she got to spend every last moment of her vacation with him, she would be a lucky woman. When he released her, she was almost disappointed.

"Ready for some dinner theatre?" he asked her.

"Dinner theatre?" Tara did not remember there being any dinner theatre on the program.

"We'll eat dinner first and then see the show, so to speak." Ryan looked as if he were keeping something from her.

"And just what kind of show are we going to see?" Tara was starting to feel a little uncomfortable.

"Something you've never seen before. Perhaps a little risqué."

Risqué? Tara nibbled on her bottom lip and reminded herself that what happened here, stayed here. She could be a completely different person and have a few adventures she wouldn't normally have. "And we're just watching?"

"Yes, unless you choose to partake."

Tara's eyes narrowed on him. "We'll see."

Her answer seemed to catch him off guard. He took her hand and started to escort her away from her room. "This way, dear Tara. We're off on a grand adventure tonight."

"If you say so," she replied. All kinds of things popped into her head. He said a show. That part was the only thing that seemed true to her. Grand adventure? She'd find out soon enough. Since they walked in silence, she had plenty of time to come up with little fantasies in her head as to what she thought might happen. By the time they made their way to a small building, Tara had herself convinced they were going to a strip show of some kind—like burlesque, but with more flesh.

When Ryan opened the door for them, Tara paused for a moment. "You're not afraid, are you?"

"No... not really. Because I can leave if I'm not comfortable, right?"

"Exactly. Just trying to show you all the things Beau Reve can offer." He grinned at her.

The problem with that was all Tara wanted to do was spend time with him, not eating. Unless she was eating something off of him. Tara bit her bottom lip as she imagined a different use for the chocolate syrup that had come with the fruit. She'd keep that in the back of her mind for later.

As they entered the room, they were escorted to a large banquet room and seated at a table for two. Tara looked around and found the walls were all covered in black velvet draperies from top to bottom. The tables were covered in black too. In fact, as she looked up and down, she noticed that everything was black.

A small platform stage was painted black, with a few stage lights overhead. On the stage was a long black couch with no back — it almost looked like a bed, but she couldn't be sure. Was that cuffs on top? Tara was starting to get a funny feeling in the pit of her stomach, and she wasn't sure whether she was disturbed or excited.

Tara let Ryan pull her chair out for her and sat down. "Thank you."

He sat down across from her. "Keep an open mind."

She crossed her arms over her chest. "What have you gotten us into?"

"Food first. Then a show." His eyes twinkled. "And you don't even have to pick the food. It just comes right out to you."

"Making fun of my lack of decision-making skills?"

"Never." He winked at her.

As they started to bring out the food, Tara saw a few men walk onto the stage. They were bare chested and wore what looked like leather kilts with silver studs. Were they naked underneath? Tara tilted her head slightly to see if any of them would move so she could get a better look.

"How's the chicken?" Ryan interrupted her perusal.

Tara blushed. "Good. So, what exactly are they doing up there?"

"Dinner theatre." He refused to give her a straight answer.

"Ryan...." Tara put her fork down. "I'm not going to eat a bite more until you tell me."

"Fine. Ruin the surprise. When the food is taken away, those guys are going to ask for a volunteer from the audience."

"For what?"

"Pleasure." He smiled slowly at her.

"We're going to watch them have sex?" Did her voice sound a little shrill?

"Nope. We're going to listen. When she goes up, the lights go off. Every once in a while, the lights will come on, just to give a peek. But for the most part, the experience is in the dark."

Tara felt her eyebrows raise in surprise. What in the actual hell had he brought her to? Tara fought the urge to run from the table. But then again, her interest was slightly piqued. "I see. So, one lucky woman gets to have sex with that group of men?"

"Not exactly. No penetration involved. Their motivation is to bring pleasure to women. No self-fulfillment."

"Oh." Her mouth was open in a large round circle right before her jaw dropped. Tara wondered what it would be like to have all those mouths and hands all over her body. "You said, women?"

"Whoever wants to give it a try."

"And you're hoping that I volunteer?" Tara crossed her arms over her chest and let out a long sigh.

"Not unless it's something you want to do." He leaned over and kissed her cheek, then her mouth. He broke the kiss and whispered, "I want to be a part of your sexual awakening, Tara."

She shivered at his words. So far, he had not disappointed her in that area. Tara didn't know how she felt about this place, but she would at least listen or watch, whichever happened first, just to see what the hype was all about. "I thought I was already awake."

"You've only just begun. There's so much more for you to learn." He lifted her hand and brought it up to his mouth. "No strings, Tara. You can stay or go. I'll not think any less of you."

"I'm game to see what it's all about. But that's probably because you make me feel safe." She hadn't meant to say that out loud. It was true, though. Ryan did make her feel safe.

"Good. Now, finish eating." He winked at her.

Tara ate quietly, and when the waiter came to take their plates, she felt an extra beat in her heart. Was that excitement? Perhaps. Fear? No. Anxiety, maybe. She just wasn't sure what to expect.

A voice broke over the speaker, "Good evening, ladies and gentlemen. Are you ready for a special treat?"

Tara heard the crowd catcall and clap, but she sat there

in silence, waiting to see what would happen next. Ryan put his hand on hers and rubbed the top her hand with his fingers. She smiled softly at him and put her other hand on top of his. "I'm fine."

The voice continued. "We need one volunteer to experience paradise."

At least six hands rose in the air. Tara was not one of them. She was not about to put herself in that situation at all. But she wasn't above seeing the rest of it play out. Who knows? Maybe she might actually enjoy it.

The men came down and picked a shorter blonde, who clapped excitedly. She let herself be escorted up to the podium and sat down on the bed. The men started to help her undress just before the lights turned off.

"Ooh.... That feels...oh!" The woman's voice rang out.

"Lay back," one of the men told her.

The next few minutes were filled with moans that were escalating quickly. The microphone picked up the sounds of lips and hands on flesh. At the ten-minute mark, a strobe light came on and showed the woman was cuffed to the bed with a man on each side. Their mouths and hands were roaming all over her body, while one of them was going down on her.

Tara shivered slightly at the provocative image before her. When the strobe lights turn off again, Tara heard moans panting from different parts of the room. What in the world?

She felt the brush of air as Ryan slid his chair by hers. His mouth whispered in her ear, "Do you like this, Tara?"

Her breath caught in her throat. Was it wrong if she admitted that she was aroused by the scene and the sounds that fluttered through the air around them?

"Tara?" His mouth nibbled on her ear lobe, and his arms slid around her stomach.

"What?" Tara felt his mouth on her skin, and his hand went lower, sliding her skirt up her leg.

"Are you enjoying the show?" He whispered again.

"*Yes,*" she answered against her better judgment.

He growled in her ear as his hand worked up her leg. When he slid his fingers under her panties, Tara shivered. "What are you doing, Ryan?"

"Helping you get the full show experience. Relax, Tara. No one can see you."

As his fingers worked her over, Tara saw the strobe light come back on. The woman was in the throes of an orgasm that looked earth-shattering, for she wrenched her body off the table. Tara's whole body was heightened with desire as Ryan brought her close to her own orgasm. His mouth captured hers and swallowed her whimper as her body shook against his hand. The lights went off again, and Ryan continued to work her over with his talented fingers. When the lights came on, he removed his hand and kissed her shoulder softly.

The woman was no longer on the stage. New men were

now standing there in her place. The voice came over the speaker. "Well, that was extraordinary. Is there anyone else who'd like a taste?"

Tara looked over at Ryan as if she were trying to determine what his thoughts were. "Do you want me to go up there, Ryan?"

His eyes flashed with desire. "That choice has to be yours."

"Would it turn you on?" She asked him.

His answer was barely audible. "*Yes.*"

Tara slowly raised her hand. She wasn't alone. When the men made their way down the stage, they stopped right before her. She wrinkled her nose at him. "You can thank me later."

"Oh, I'll definitely thank you." His sexy grin made her aware he already had plans.

Tara walked up to the stage and smiled at the men who were surrounding her. They were all very attractive men. Tara looked out at Ryan and ignored the rest of the people in the room.

As the men removed her clothing, Tara shivered in anticipation. Ryan's face looked hard and determined. He was definitely aroused. Tara smiled softly at him, and the lights went off.

Tara felt herself being led back to the couch. She laid on it and shivered as the new cool sheets were cold against her skin. Her hands and feet were cuffed to the bed, and one of them whispered in her ear.

"Are you okay?"

"Yes," she answered.

"If you want this to stop, just say so at any time. Our job is to bring you infinite pleasure. Are you ready?"

"Yes."

Tara sighed as a mouth kissed against her cheek. Hands seemed to be everywhere at once as soft caresses covered her body. She felt a tongue slide against her breast and another on the other side. The two men took her into their mouths and started to suckle them as if they were looking for fresh milk. Tara felt two hands push her legs aside as a mouth made its way to her nether regions. The soft silky tongue lapped against her clit.

Her breath caught in her throat as hands, mouths, and tongues took their fill of her. A moan was trapped in her throat, but as her desire climbed, it released so loud she was surprised at herself. When a finger slipped inside her, Tara shook around it as an orgasm ripped through her.

The men pleasured her over and over until Tara could no longer remember where she was or how she'd gotten there. She barely even noticed when the strobe lights came on — all she could focus on was the immense pleasure that was floating through her body. Tara actually lost track of all of the times she finished; however, none of them were nearly as good as what she'd had with Ryan, a fact she'd make sure to tell him afterward.

When it was over, they helped her up from the couch and ushered her through an opening in the curtains behind them. A door opened, and she was escorted inside. Tara did not speak a word to the men as they took their leave. Her clothes were folded on a dresser near the wall. She blinked in confusion for a moment, trying to get her bearings.

A voice whispered near her shoulder. "Let me help you, Tara."

Tara turned to see Ryan behind her. She wrapped her arms around him and kissed him deeply. "Thank you."

He gave her a sexy grin. "I thought you'd like it."

"It was definitely an experience." She stepped into the panties that Ryan held up for her.

"Yes, it was." His mouth kissed the back of her neck and pulled her back against him. She felt his erection behind her, hard as a rock. "God, I want you, but not here."

She nibbled on her lip as he slid the dress over her head, his thumbs tweaking her nipples through the material when it settled over her. She whimpered and sunk back against him. "There's only one problem."

"What's that?" He asked with a husky whisper.

"They weren't you."

She turned in his arms and was surprised by the fervor of his kiss. Tara wasn't sure how long the kiss went on, but when it was broken, a spell had been woven over. She wanted him more than the air she breathed.

"Come with me, Tara."

He led her from the room out into the cool night air that felt refreshing on her skin. She had no idea where he was leading her, but if it meant she'd end up in his arms tonight, she'd follow him to the fiery pits of hell.

Chapter 14

They spoke very little as Ryan led her back to his bungalow. She couldn't quite form words yet, not ones that made sense. Her legs were still trembling slightly as they walked, a point she hoped he did not notice. Clearly, she had been affected by the dinner theatre, well before she became a participant. Never before had she ever let herself do something so risqué.

What was Amelia going to say? Should she tell her? Or was that too much information? Part of her wanted to, just because she wanted to compare notes on their experiences. The good news was she had faced a new challenge, and while she was not completely unscathed, it hadn't been nearly as hard to get through it as she thought it might be.

Tara was still trying to examine her motives for volunteering. She wanted to please Ryan, to make him as wild and crazy as she felt inside every time he was near her. But in the end, that performance had been about trying something new, something that she would never have tried before. That was the point of Beau Reve, to live a little and either explore a fantasy you had or inspire one that might not have existed before.

Ryan opened his door and escorted her inside. He still had not said a word to her. Tara wondered what he was thinking. He had seemed to be enjoying the show, but there was something hidden deeper inside that he wasn't sharing.

"Is something wrong?" She asked him.

"Why do you ask?" He answered a little tersely.

"You seem upset. Did I do something wrong?" Tara started to worry that maybe volunteering had been a bad idea. The time that had passed between the actual event and now was brief, yet a wide void seemed to extend between them.

"No," he denied.

"You're angry." Tara stepped closer to him and put her hand on his face. Was he ashamed of her now? He had been the one to encourage her. That couldn't be it. Could he be…? No…he couldn't be jealous, could he? She put her hands on his face and brought her face up to kiss his. He didn't deny her.

When she broke the kiss, she walked away from him, not quite sure what to say in this particular situation. "They were amateurs compared to you. All I could think about was you."

Her words seemed to break through his fog. He moved closer to her, reminding her of a predator searching for its prey. Ryan reached out and pulled her closer to him. "I hated them for loving you when I have no claim to you at all."

"I know. We both know what this is, Ryan."

"I don't want anyone else to have you," he growled as he kissed her hard and fast.

Tara pushed him away and backed up slightly. "Don't say things you'll regret, Ryan."

She didn't know where he was going with all this, but Tara didn't want him to make some kind of declaration that would melt away the minute she stepped on the airplane that would lead her home. That would only lead to heartache that she didn't need in her life. Tara was not looking for any kind of relationship in her life, especially now that her eyes were opening to a whole different world around her. While she was interested in learning more about her sexuality, Tara wasn't prepared to explore it with any other men on this island. She trusted him to teach her things that had been left out of her education so far.

"I want you, Tara. I've never wanted another woman like I want you," he whispered as if he were tortured.

"You can have me here, Ryan." Tara lowered her dress down her body and slid her panties down her legs. "Take me."

"God, you're beautiful." He pulled her against him again. This time his mouth covered hers in a softer kiss as his hands caressed her back.

"You're not bad yourself," she said when he broke the kiss. She pushed her hands under his shirt and removed it in between kisses. Tara worked on his shorts with the same finesse. She pulled him by the hand to the bedroom behind them, not even worrying about walking naked through his bungalow. All she cared about was getting as close to him as she could.

She lay down on the bed and crooked a finger at him. "Come here, Ryan."

He gave her a sexy smile before he joined her on the bed. When his mouth distracted her, his hands roamed over her breasts. When his fingers ran across her nipples, Tara felt like purring. Unlike the other men, an electric jolt shot through her body wherever he touched. Her body craved him like no other.

Removing his mouth from hers, his mouth worked its way down her body. His lips took her left nipple into his mouth while his hand played with her right. Before she knew it, the gentle sucking became intense. He nibbled on her nipple, then switched to the other. Tara looked down at her swollen nipple and was surprised at how engorged it appeared. While she had enjoyed what the men had done to her, this was bliss. She ached in places that never ached before.

When his hand moved down to stroke her clit, Tara thought she had died and gone to heaven, if girls who did naughty things like this were allowed inside its Pearly Gates. Tonight, she was a very naughty girl, and she was his.

"Say it, Tara."

"Say what?" She didn't know what he was asking from her.

"My name." He sucked her nipples into his mouth so hard, Tara gasped aloud.

She blinked, dumbfounded. "Your name?"

"Yes. Say it, Tara."

He continued to suck on her breasts, and she moaned again. "Ryan!"

He bit her hard on the nipple, and she pushed his head closer to her chest. Tara loved the way he feasted on her flesh. When he shoved his finger deep into her, she whimpered against him.

"Did they do it like this, Tara?" He asked her.

"No...."

"Was it hard?" He pushed his fingers deep and hard inside her.

"No...."

Ryan stopped his movements and pulled his fingers out. She whimpered at the loss. He kissed her softly on the lips, and she sighed against him. "Please don't stop," she begged him.

"You want more, Tara?"

His eyes were on fire with desire as his fingers slid inside her again. Ryan seemed to have a much wilder side tonight, one that was driving further than she was used to. Tara wasn't afraid of him. As his finger took every inch of her, Tara felt an orgasm just beneath the surface. His mouth was back on her breasts, sucking and biting her as she shivered in bliss beneath him. Tara had no defense against the combination of his mouth and hands. She came hard and fast against his hand.

Ryan released her breasts and pulled his fingers out of her wet core. "Don't worry, Tara. I'm not done. I'm going to make you beg for more."

"Oh?" That sounded delicious.

Ryan leaned over and kissed her on the lips once before kneeling before her. He spread her legs wider and delved within the folds between her legs. When he brought his mouth to her clit, his tongue snaked across it, and Tara felt a tremor of excitement race through her. So soft, like a sweet, gentle massage, his tongue stroked her with much more heat than the men who had pleasured her before. Her body only wanted what he could give her. Before she knew it, her insides were quaking, her legs trembled, and an orgasm ripped through her.

When he stuck a finger into her, Tara fought the urge to wrench herself from the bed. She wanted him so bad that she was gripping the bed with her toes and her hands. When he took her over and over with his hand and his masterful tongue, Tara was thrashing like a wild banshee beneath him. She thought of nothing but how good it would feel to have his large cock pressing deep inside her. With the mere thought of it, the more her thoughts sent her spiraling to another finish. His name left her lips, and Ryan growled into her skin. He bit her clit and pushed up away from her.

"That sounded like a good one, Tara. Are you ready for more?"

"More?" She barely got the word out. Tara could barely think, her brain was so muddled with the desirous fog he had built around her. She'd lost count of how many orgasms she'd had earlier, yet Ryan seemed to be on a mission to top the charts. He must be comparing himself to the group of men.

"Yes, more."

His eyes were like a stormy sea. Tara could tell that Ryan was holding back, mastering his own desire to bring her infinite pleasure. When he slid his fingers back into her wet heat, she rode against them. He moved them around inside until he found a spot that made her want to rip his hand away. What the hell was that? It was pleasure and pain at the same time, and Tara couldn't decide which feeling would win over, but as Ryan continued to move across that spot, a wild, crazy fire built inside her.

"Oh, my God!" Before she could help herself, Tara was a wild woman beneath him. All she could think about was

Ryan slamming deep within her, so hard and tight the way he had on the boat.

"Say it, Tara."

"Please, Ryan!"

"Please, what?"

"Fuck me! Please!" Her words had hit on desperation. She wanted him so badly it made her sick to her stomach to think about it.

He paused for a moment to retrieve the protection he had brought to the bed with him. When Ryan was ready, he moved over her and plunged deep inside her. His cock stretched her slowly at first, then his fast movements took over. He reached beneath her and grabbed her ass with his hands. He squeezed her flesh painfully as he used the angle to drive deeper into her. Ryan may have seemed like a gentleman last night, but he was pure fantasy lover right now, one who was competing with a fantasy that could never compare to him. Tara was enjoying every minute of it. She wrapped her legs around him and pulled him deep inside her. She met each pump of his hips as Ryan continued to take her fast and hard.

"Oh, yes! That's right, Tara." He jerked against her one last time and collapsed over her.

She couldn't help thinking how much she had really missed out in life. If she had just tried to find someone who made her pulse race before now, she could have been sexually satisfied a long time ago. She hadn't been ready then, but she certainly was now.

Ryan rolled away from her and pulled her into his arms. She lay there in the aftermath, his arms stroking her back. Tara wondered if it had been good for him too. How did she compare to all the women he'd had up until this point? Did she even want to know the answer to that? She barely knew him. She had no right to be jealous of his past, present, or future.

"That was amazing," she whispered.

He chuckled, and she looked up at him. "You drive me crazy, Tara."

"I do?" she asked him innocently. Maybe taking part in the dinner show had done something for him after all, once he got over all the jealousy. Jealousy that she didn't quite understand really. He came here as often as he pleased. He'd had how many women in the past? Surely, she couldn't compare to all of them.

"You do, and unfortunately, this will have to take a slight detour."

"What do you mean?" Tara had a bad feeling about this.

"I have to go for a few days. But I will come back before you leave," he promised her.

"Oh." She tried to hide her disappointment.

"Two days tops. I have some business I need to attend to." He kissed her shoulder. "I wish I could stay."

"Me too," she whispered hollowly. She wasn't counting

on feeling so sad at his news. Was she getting too attached to him? That was a bad idea. Maybe she should distance herself a little bit. Perhaps this break was exactly what they needed because if she grew too close to him, she would have trouble leaving in the end. "The island will be boring without you."

He chuckled. "Beau Reve is anything but boring."

So, he said, but honestly, he had given her the courage to explore. Tara wasn't sure she would be able to do much without him here. She'd probably hit the beach and read her book or layout by her pool. Maybe she'd see if Abby was around. She actually liked spending time with her. She'd fill up her time with as much as she could before he came back to her.

Tara sighed when he pulled her closer. Her eyes fluttered annoyingly, and she tried to fight the sleepiness that was flowing through her limbs. Her body had been through a lot tonight. Tara's body gave in, and she fell asleep against him.

Chapter 15

The next morning Tara woke in an empty bed and panicked slightly. Had he left without even saying goodbye? Should it really matter to her? What actual claim did she have over him? None. And this was precisely why she should not have gotten involved with him.

Tara pushed the covers aside and went in search of her clothes. That was when she heard the shower running. She breathed a sigh of relief and decided to do something out of the norm for herself. Walking into the bathroom, Tara saw him standing in the glass shower. She took in his backside as he was turned away from her.

Would he want her to join him? Tara felt a little bit of doubt creep into her thoughts, but then tossed it out the window. There was only one way to find out. Tara opened the shower stall and slid in behind him. "Good morning."

He turned to smile at her. "I was trying to let you sleep.

You had a long night."

"So, did you," she smiled at him.

"The best kind." He wrapped his arms around her and pulled her naked body against him.

"I wasn't sure if I should interrupt your shower." Tara smiled up at him and offered her mouth up for a kiss.

"Any morning I find a beautiful woman in my shower is a good morning, Tara."

Any woman would do, though, right? She couldn't help the thoughts that were swarming through her head. For her, it was already clear that her body wanted his more than any man she'd ever been with before. Now, though, was not the time to be thinking about that. Not when Ryan's mouth came down to hers.

Pulling away from his kiss, Tara let her eyes travel up and down his beautiful body. Ryan worked out, and it was easy to see. Every inch of him was chiseled perfection. She especially loved that he was already fully aroused this morning. She licked her lips and thought about what it would feel like to put her mouth to good use on his cock.

Tara let herself explore his wet body. Her lips trailed kisses down his body as she licked some of the water away. Spicy and sweet. When she knelt down before him, Tara took his cock into her mouth.

Ryan groaned and steadied himself on the walls of the shower. "Well, this is a great way to start the morning."

Her reply was to suck him hard into her mouth while

she cupped his balls in her hand. Tara took his entire length into her mouth and was surprised how much fit. She licked the base of his cock with her tongue and let it circle around him as she released him. She had never enjoyed going down on a man before today, but with such a handsome model in front of her, it was hard to not want to wrap her hands and mouth around him.

She continued to work him over until Ryan pushed her head away from him and had a slightly dangerous look to his face. "If you keep that up, there'll be nothing left for you."

She pouted at him and stood up. "You're not that easy, are you?"

"For a hot sexy woman sucking me off, hell yeah. Every man's fantasy, Tara. Stand up."

She stood up as he commanded and looked at him for her next direction. She had learned that following his directions led to very pleasurable things, and with only a week to learn from him, Tara wanted him to master every inch of her body.

His eyes softened once before his wicked gleam returned, "Ever have sex in the shower before, Tara?"

"No." It was a whisper. Tara wondered what he had in mind, but before she could ask, he lifted one of her legs and slid it around his ass. He moved her closer to the wall, and she gripped the bar above her head, which until now she hadn't noticed. Brass rings were settled at different parts of the wall, making her think that these showers had definitely been made with sex in mind.

"Stand still, Tara."

She braced herself for his next actions, as his hot cock slid inside her. The heat of his shaft made her crave the end she knew she would find. The fact that he had not worn protection made her even wilder than usual. She was not afraid of the consequences, for she was already taking prevention.

When he started to pump into her, she grasped the rings above her head. Over and over, he plunged into her, and when she thought she could bear it no more, her orgasm sent her over the edge. Tara arched her back, and his mouth planted firmly on her breast. He sucked her nipple hard, and she fought the urge to push him away. Her nipples were still sensitive from the night before. She came so hard and fast she thought she would crash to the floor on top of him, but he held her tight. Before she knew it, Ryan's cum trickled down her leg to be washed away by the hot steamy water that fell down upon them.

Ryan let her legs down and kissed her hard upon the mouth. Tara wrapped her hands around his head and pulled him closer. "You are some kind of wonderful."

Ryan grinned and swatted her on the ass. "Time to get moving, Tara. I have a plane to catch."

"Too bad." Did she look as crestfallen as she felt? She hoped not. It wasn't as if Ryan had told her that he wanted no one else but her. He was here for the same reason as everyone else, right? And she was pretty sure they had both established there were no strings involved.

"It's not another woman, Tara."

"Should that matter? We both said no strings, Ryan. Although I would have a problem with all of this if you were married. I would hate to be a homewrecker."

"I'm not that kind of man." He helped her step out of the shower and held up a towel.

"Never married?"

"No. Just haven't been focused on that part of my life." He was toweling himself off.

"Me either. I've been too busy making sure my brothers made it through puberty." She grinned at him as she dried herself off. "I don't even know if I'm ready for that. I'm only twenty-five. My biological clock is still on snooze mode."

"Men are lucky. We don't seem to have that internal clock. Although, it would be nice to have someone to come home to."

"I'm sure you have your share of women to keep you warm," she teased him.

"Not as many as you'd think. A handful here and there. They all seem to want the same thing, though."

"Money? Prestige? Social standing?" Tara was thinking about Sienna and Rachel. Those two were probably exactly like the ones that threw themselves at him.

"Exactly."

"Does money even make you happy?" Tara asked him.

"Sometimes. Other times, no. But I seem to make more of it each year."

"Oh, what a problem," she teased him.

"Hey, it can be. I never know who is being real with me or artificial."

"I can understand that. The funny thing is the women chasing after you never had to live with little. They probably don't really appreciate your money the way they should." Where money was concerned, Tara just wanted to be able to support herself and help her siblings whenever they needed help. Those were her only goals.

"And what would you do if you had billions of dollars, Tara?" He asked her.

"Me?" She nibbled on her lip and thought for a minute. "I guess I would spend it on ways to help others who needed help. I'd help my family first. I really don't need a pile of money. I just need a job that pays me enough to take care of myself, so no one else has to."

"And then what?" He asked her.

"I'd find a way to help women who needed a hand up. I used to volunteer at a domestic abuse shelter. Their stories are heartbreaking."

Tara found Ryan looking at her thoughtfully as if he had not expected her answers.

"Were you ever abused?"

"No. My aunt was, though. She didn't make it out in

time. We were pretty close. I lost her when I was ten."

"I'm sorry. Any man who raises his hand to a woman or child is no man at all." Ryan shook his head in disgust. "You are certainly refreshing."

"How do you mean?" Tara was perplexed.

"Most people I ask that question to talk about the fancy house or car they'd buy. The people they'd meet. The status they'd have."

Tara shuddered at the thought. "That would never be me. You'd have to drag me to social events."

"But you'd go."

What was he talking about? Tara found his questions a little unusual this morning. "If it was supporting the man I loved, yes, I would. Love gives you courage to do things you wouldn't normally do." Tara found herself blushing because she realized how profound her words truly were. She was falling for him, even though she was trying not to do just that.

"I suppose that's true." Ryan looked at his phone and cursed. "Damn it. I have to go. Don't leave Beau Reve before I come back. I'll come as soon as I can. I had to bring some work with me, unfortunately. Not all of us leave it all behind."

"Of course. Well, I guess I'll just spend some quiet time to myself. I brought a few books. I'm kind of tired anyway."

He pulled her close to him. "If I could spend every second with you, I'd be a lucky man, Tara."

"I think I'd be the lucky one, Ryan." She smiled at him and kissed him on the cheek. "Come get me when you want me, Ryan."

Now that she was completely dressed, Tara was ready to go too. She left as soon as he did and made her way back to her room. As she did, she realized that her life was changing in ways she could not completely understand. Sex had never been this exciting for her before. Not to mention the magnetic pull she felt for Ryan. All of it defied reason. She would just have to hold out until the end, take whatever she could before her time ended here. That was easier said than done.

Chapter 16

Tara spent the rest of the day by herself, which she actually needed. She'd had more activity the previous day than she was used to. While she was used to being alone, Tara was not able to find the peace she usually found. Ryan's easy companionship was something that she had not expected. Sure, there was a fair amount of sex in there too, but she didn't feel like she had to prove anything when she was around him. That was nice for a change.

Tara had a lot of things to try to figure out for herself. Would she look for someone like Ryan when she left Beau Reve, someone who made her feel alive? Tara was afraid that it would be hard to find someone who measured up. It had absolutely nothing to do with his money, but his willingness to put her needs first. She had never been with a man whose mission was to make sure his partner was completely satisfied before he took what he wanted. It was refreshing and would be hard to find. How would she go about doing that? Random sex with different men? That wasn't usually her thing, but clearly, she had been missing out.

Sighing, Tara finished getting dressed. She still wasn't sure when Ryan was going to return. He had said two days, but then who knew how long his business would actually take him? Nothing was ever a guarantee. Even if he did return, would he come right back to her? Or had he gotten everything he had wanted from her? Tara was just one woman in a long string of them.

"Why do you do this to yourself?" Tara asked the reflection in the mirror. "No strings."

No strings...yet there was a part of her that screamed inside that she wanted those strings, even if he didn't. But she wouldn't press the issue. She was too proud for that. All she had to do was come up with a way to distract herself until he returned.

Today she was going to head to the large pool on the west side. It had a large spa attached to it that she might try out. Maybe she'd get her nails done for a change. She was certainly high strung. She'd check in with them when she headed over there and see what they had available.

When she made her way to the pool, she found a familiar face. Abby waved her over to her. "Good morning, Tara."

"Morning, Abby." Tara smiled at her. "Is this seat free?"

"Sure. Pull up a lounger. I'd love the company."

Tara set her bag down on the ground and found a seat next to Abby. "How is the sun today?"

"Warm enough, I suppose. It feels a little chillier than usual."

"I think it's gorgeous here." Tara sighed. What would she give to live here full time like Abby? Or at least part of the time. Tara didn't much care for the winter, but she did like spring and fall, so moving to a place without them would probably make her a little homesick. Plus, she wouldn't be there for when her brothers returned home. If they chose to. They might decide to do something else for themselves.

"So, I've been thinking a lot about what we talked about the last time." Abby tugged at her wide-brimmed hat when the wind started to pull at it.

"Oh?" Tara was trying to think of which part she was talking about.

"You mentioned your jackass boss."

"Oh, yeah. He's definitely a piece of work." Tara shook her head.

"I've decided to put him out of business." Abby grinned at her.

"I'm sorry?" Tara was confused by her words. What was she talking about?

"You talked about upscale, treating the women with respect. I think there's a need for something like that. So, hear me out. Picture this—sexy women dressed in elegant wear as they serve."

"Like ball gowns?" Tara asked her curiously.

"Not exactly, but cocktail dresses perhaps. Still show some skin, but let the servers feel comfortable and confident enough to want to work there. There would be a handful of men in the bar, just to make sure the women were being treated correctly."

"How would that work?" Tara had trouble picturing it. What man would want to go to a bar where they would actually have to be accountable for their actions?

"You'd be surprised the kind of crowd it would attract."

"Really? Most of the men who come to the bar right now are men who want to spend the bare minimum and treat women however they want to."

"Yes, but with my connections darling, you'll get an entirely different clientele."

"So, you want to buy his bar?"

"Nope. I want you to build a new one."

"But I'm not qualified to do that." Tara felt like her mouth was standing wide open. Why would Abby want to give her this opportunity? What could she personally get out of it? What if she failed? How in the world would she even begin to do something like this?

"You know the ins and outs of being an employee at one of these places. You've seen what practices work and which don't."

"That's true. The women are paid below minimum wage and still have to split some of their tips. Also, Lane charges full prices for watered-down beverages. No insurance. But we do get vacation days, which are paid at a much lower rate than other places."

"So?"

"So what?" Tara was still confused about all of this.

"I've already had them looking for possible properties in your area. Would you consider being the manager?"

"I…. Yes. I would. I'm not sure that I have the skills you need, though, Abby."

"Skills, schmills. You have more inside you than you think, darling. I've read your file. Raising teenage boys, keeping your family together. You have wonderful credit, which means you have always kept your finances stable. Not many people your age have been able to do that. Besides, I've got enough investors interested that would be happy to start breaking ground before the end of the year."

Tara stared at Abby like she was in some kind of dream. "I just...I don't understand, Abby. I don't know what to say."

"You're welcome, Tara. I believe in giving people a step up when they need one. You need one, dear. I was there once myself, love. I'd like for you to come to Beau Reve quarterly to give me updates."

"I get to come back here?" Tara smiled brightly.

"You like it here, then?"

171

"Yes. It's heaven."

"And Ryan?"

Tara sighed. "Honestly, I've never had this much sex in my life."

Abby laughed. "Beau Reve will do that to you."

"Yes. I find I'm rather insatiable." Tara giggled.

"You should join me at the peek show tonight," Abby suggested.

"What is a peek show?" Tara was almost afraid to hear the answer.

"I find watching others have sex is quite an adventure, even if it means I don't get to have it at the time."

"You like being a voyeur?" Tara put her hand over her mouth and closed her eyes. "I didn't mean for that to come out the way it sounded."

"Most people enjoy watching, Tara. There's nothing to apologize for. I often forget that not everyone has had the exciting life that I have."

"I might like that." Tara had enjoyed listening to the theatre show the other night, and even more when she could see the bits and pieces in between. It was like a live porno, something she could not take her eyes off while she had been there. "We went to the dinner theatre."

"How was that, Tara?" Abby asked her curiously.

Tara blushed. "I had a *real* good time."

"Did you volunteer?"

"Yes, I did. I thought it would turn Ryan on."

"I'm sure it sent his blood pressure skyrocketing. For whatever reason, men have trouble watching their women being pleasured by other men."

"He did seem a little upset after. I had to reassure him that they were nothing like him. I've never met a man like him before." Tara sighed. Her body already missed his touch.

"You've got it bad." Abby wrinkled her nose.

Tara looked down at the ground. "I do. I was trying to fight it, but the feelings are there."

"It's only natural to get attached to the man who brings about your sexual revolution. I was attached to my first man too. Then there was the fifth one—he took me even further than I thought I could go. Introduced me to some ménage. Now that is definitely my favorite thing."

Ménage? As in multiple partners? Tara could see the fascination with that. Had she allowed the men on the stage to go further with her, she might have found that equally as satisfying. Imagining Ryan in the mix with them—now that made her want that even more. He would have upped the ante quite a bit. "That does sound intriguing."

"You never know what you'll like until you try it." Abby winked at her. "So, darling girl, you return home soon. I have an investor who would like to meet with you when you get home. We want to break ground as soon as we can."

A high-end night club, where women were treated like

queens even when they were on duty. Tara would have to figure out the ropes to running a place like that. "There's so much I don't know about running a club, Abby."

"I'm not going to throw you to the wolves, Tara. I've got the perfect partner ready to help you through it. You'll be trained in no time. And he'll check in on you from time to time." Abby smiled secretively, and Tara couldn't help wondering what in the world she was up to.

"I hope I don't let you down, Abby."

"I doubt you could. The risk is worth the attempt, Tara. Don't ever forget that. I'm having a package sent to your room later today with the details you'll need."

"How did you get this done in just a few days?" Tara couldn't believe this was happening so quickly.

"Money makes the world go round. You'd be surprised what you can accomplish when you have an excess. One day you'll know too."

"I seriously doubt that." Tara chuckled.

"I intend to make you a partner, dear girl. The success of this venture could very well make you enough money to be set for life."

"I...I don't know what to say, Abby." There were probably ten thousand more people who were more qualified to be brought in on a project like this. She didn't understand why Abby felt she was the person for the job. Tara tried to fight off the negative thoughts that were already filtering in, like what if she ruined the opportunity and the club completely tanked?

"Just take the opportunity, Tara. You can't be afraid of failure."

"I will." She couldn't promise success, but that didn't mean she would plan on failure either.

"Good. Now, I'm off to see a man about a massage. We'll meet at the Carter building later. I believe the peep show is scheduled for seven."

"Can't wait." And she couldn't. She was actually curious as to what she might see in the show. Would it be a ménage? A couple? Same sex? Any of that would be entertaining to her. She had promised Amelia that she would live a little. She planned to fulfill that promise to her best ability. The only thing she was missing right now was Ryan.

Tara watched Abby leave and wondered how in the world her life had turned around this much in a matter of days. Amelia was not going to believe it! Although she wasn't sure who she was allowed to tell about the new club. They'd still have to figure out what to call it. There were so many details that would have to be ironed out. Tara was excited and nervous about the opportunity. It meant a different future for herself than she had ever imagined. Life was beginning to look up for a change. Now, she was half-tempted to return to her room and start searching business models that would work for the club. One thing at a time, though. For now, she was going to soak up the rays and relax. Who knew what the evening would bring?

Chapter 17

When the evening finally came, Tara made her way to the Carter building and looked for the signs that would lead her to the peep show. She was relieved when she found Abby waiting outside for her.

"Ready for a show, Tara?"

"I sure hope so." Tara was still imagining all kinds of scenarios in her head.

"Come with me." Abby grabbed her arm and pulled her inside.

Tara was led into a large room with movie theatre recliners. It reminded her of a home studio one might have in their basement. Three of the walls were covered in the same darkening velvet as the dinner theatre. The fourth wall was a large two-sided mirror. Tara couldn't see in the room as the lights were out.

"Don't worry. The show hasn't started yet. I'm not sure

who the lineup is, but there are three rooms on the other side of that mirror."

"Three?" Tara felt her eyebrows rise curiously.

"Yep. Three beautiful scenes at once, my dear. Constant action, and when they finish, new people come in to replace them." Abby shivered visibly as if she were excited.

Tara appreciated her fervor for it. She hoped she enjoyed it as much as her friend did. She was certainly heading into it with an open mind. "Can they see us?"

"Yes."

"Really?" Tara found that curious.

"They like to be watched, my dear. It drives their excitement up. I've done it a few times myself. Now I find it more enjoyable to watch."

"This should be interesting." Tara giggled nervously. She wasn't sure how she felt that the others could see them. It was like being a kid caught with her hand in the cookie jar. Tara was glad they weren't in the first row of seats. Perhaps she could slink down in her chair a little.

The lights turned on in the rooms, and three separate couples were inside. Tara found it hard to focus on all of them at once, so she decided to look at them one at a time. That was far easier.

In the first room, a man was standing naked with a woman at his feet. Tara could not see the woman at all, for her head was placed in his crotch. Tara saw the slow bob of her head and realized the woman was sucking him in her mouth. The man was slowly getting into it. As the woman continued to work her magic on him, his hand came down to her head and pushed her harder against him. Tara saw the woman bring her hands up to cup his balls in her hands. The chords in his neck strained right before she finished sucking him off completely. The lights turned off in that room, which probably meant that they would be switching the couple out.

In the second room, there was a woman being pleasured by two men. One was going down on her, while the other was sucking on her breasts. The woman looked up at the window to see if anyone was watching and smiled at the room. Tara knew exactly how that felt, although there had been more than two men on the stage. She could see the draw for that. When the first man stood up and shoved deep inside her, Tara's breath caught in her throat. As the woman took the other man's cock into her mouth, Tara's face flushed with heat. They were all enjoying themselves. That was easy to see.

In the third room, Tara saw a woman tied to some kind of stand. There was a man standing before her who she thought looked familiar, but she couldn't quite place him. He was running his hands and mouth up and down the woman, who was tied in place. The brunette was definitely enjoying the attention. Tara could hear her moans from here. When the man picked up a vibrating dildo and pushed it inside her, the woman rode it in ecstasy. He removed it and replaced it with his mouth, pleasuring her without any mechanical assistance. Then he stood up and turned around, and Tara gasped aloud.

"Ryan?"

He must have heard her, for he looked through the mirror. When he saw her sitting there, his eyes flashed with something that looked like regret. Tara closed her eyes and tried to school the expression on her face. She turned to Abby. "I think I'm done, Abby."

"Are you all right, dear?"

Tara gave her a feeble smile and lied. "Yes. I just...I can't watch this."

Tara didn't even look to see if Ryan was watching her leave. At this point, it didn't matter. He had lied to her. She had no right to anything with him, not really, but she hadn't expected him to make up some lie just so he could get away from her.

"Come with me, Tara." Abby led her out of the room and took her hand. "Why don't you stay with me tonight?"

Tara gave her an appreciative smile. "Thank you. I think that's a good idea. I just don't want to face him right now."

"I've got plenty of room, and I have those papers for you." Abby patted her arm. "Men can be assholes sometimes, Tara."

"Yes, I guess so, but I didn't really have any expectations of a future with him, Abby. I just wish he wouldn't have felt the need to lie. I could have handled the truth. This... this is so much worse."

"Yes, I agree. And it's not like him at all." Abby made a clucking sound with her tongue. "Maybe I was wrong about him."

Tara followed her into her building and was surprised to find the entire building was all her house. It had just looked like the other buildings that separated into several condo-like areas. "This is beautiful."

"It's enough," smiled Abby. "Now, come come. Let's have a drink and bitch about men who have no common sense at all."

"I made a mistake, Abby."

Tara sighed and fought the sting of tears that wanted to fall down her face. Her heart was breaking, even though she had tried to build walls around it. She was head over heels for a man who clearly had no problem sleeping with any woman. The only thing that could have made it worse was for it to be Sienna, who had almost thrown herself at him on the beach. Of course, now she wondered how many women he had been sleeping with all along while he was playing with her before they even had sex.

"What is that?"

"I fell in love. I should have known better." Her lips wobbled slightly as she fought back a gulp.

"Oh, dear, yes. I can see that now." Abby offered her arms to her. "Come here, love. Let's get that cried out. You don't want to keep that bottled up."

Tara let her comfort her as the tears continued to fall. How could she have been so stupid? She had done things with him, for him even, things that she would never have done. Now the entire thing was tainted with his lie. "I don't think I want to return to my room."

"Don't want to see him?" Abby asked perceptively.

"No. He told me he was going to be working. Working, Abby. Why did he have to be so wonderful and then turn around and...?"

"I wish I knew, dear girl. You're welcome to stay here with me."

"Thank you, but I think I might just want to go home." Tara wasn't sure staying here was something she wanted to do now.

"Don't do that, Tara. He wins then. You can't let him win. Let him see you having fun. Show him that your life does not revolve around him," Abby encouraged her.

"I'm not sure I can, Abby." Tara didn't trust herself around him.

"I understand. Maybe next time you come here, you can find a few different partners," Abby suggested.

"Maybe." Tara sighed. "Don't worry, I'm not going to think about him when I get home. Screw him. He's just another jackass pretending to be a gentleman. He can go fuck himself."

"Yes, that's the spirit," Abby cheered her on.

"Can you help me get home sooner?" Tara asked her.

"I can, but I think you shouldn't let him ruin your vacation."

"This has still been one of the best experiences of my life, Abby. One jerk is not going to stain it. Plus, it's the start of a beautiful friendship."

Which was more important. The opportunities that Abby was offering her would more than make up for the heartache she felt right now. Time would change that; Tara was sure of it. Someday she would be able to forget the handsome man who had brought her to life in ways she had never expected. Tara had never known how much she was missing out on before.

"I'll have the bellhop go pack your stuff for you and bring it here." Abby picked up her phone and started to text someone. "Done."

"I'm sorry, Abby."

"What are you sorry for, dear child?" Abby looked at her with concern.

"I ruined your night." Tara sighed sadly.

"Bah. There will be other nights. I just wish one asshole didn't send you packing."

"I'm coming back, though, right?" Tara reminded her.

"Yes, every quarter. Speaking of which, here is the project plan." Abby handed her a binder full of information.

"How in the world did you have this put together so quickly?" Tara still could not believe all of this was happening. She thumbed through the pages and saw a tentative sketch here and there. It certainly made it seem more real to her.

"I had a lot of time on my hands. And when you have resources at your fingertips, you can make the world turn faster."

"You've got a lot of great ideas here so far."

"Yes, but I still expect plenty of input from you. You've worked in the industry. Different jobs, too, it seems."

"Yes. That's true." Although lately, the most she had done was on the serving end. Tara was still hopeful that her experiences would be valuable.

"Remember, the sky is the limit."

"I will. I see there are a few contact numbers in here." Tara would make a personal note to keep that information memorized and ready for any time she needed it.

"Yes, and the man I want you to work with will be contacting you a little later."

Something mysterious crossed over Abby's face as if she were leaving something important out. Tara tried not to read too much into it. With the way her mind was working right now, chances were she was just jumping to conclusions.

"Why don't you rest? I just got confirmation of your flight in the morning. While I'm sorry to see you go, I do understand how you feel. Next time you come to Beau Reve, I'll make sure you're well taken care of, dear."

"Thank you, Abby. For everything. There are not enough words to express my gratitude." Tara hugged her and stepped back.

"There's a guestroom at the top of the stairs, dear. Make yourself at home. Your flight is early in the morning."

Tara nodded at her and made her way up to the guest bedroom. When she climbed into the bed, she let herself cry out the rest of her frustrations. As much as she hated to admit it, this was going to be really hard to get over. Tara couldn't remember the last time her heart hurt this much. It wasn't like she had any claim over him, but his lies had broken the fantasy he had woven around her just like a needle pricking a balloon. Everything burst, and now she was trying to figure out what the next step was for her. Besides putting every minute into creating the new club, Tara would simply have to keep herself occupied so she wouldn't think about him too often. That was going to be the challenge of a lifetime. She closed her eyes and attempted to fall asleep, but it was well past midnight when she finally did.

Chapter 18

After having only a few hours of sleep, Tara woke up and got ready for her flight back to reality. When she walked downstairs, she found her bags were already sitting by the door. Abby was already up too.

"Good morning, Abby." Tara greeted her with a weak smile.

"Get any sleep?"

"Not really, but I can sleep on the plane."

"Well, I've got something for you." Abby handed her an envelope.

"What is this?" She reached for it and was almost afraid to open. When she did, she found a check for ten thousand dollars. "Abby! What is this for?"

"A paycheck, my dear. I don't want you returning to that horrible place. I need you refreshed for when you meet with my contractor. That might take some time, so until then, you can spend your time researching."

"I can't wait to start coming up with some ideas. I already thought of a potential name for the club."

"Which is?" Abby asked curiously.

"Coquette." She smiled and waited to see what Abby thought.

"I actually like that. We'll ask the others what they think at our first meeting."

"Are you going to be there?" Tara sure hoped so. She would love to work with Abby on this together. Tara had a feeling that she could learn a lot from Abby.

"Of course. But we've got time for that, my dear." Abby gestured to the bags. "A pity you're leaving, but I understand your reasons."

"Time to get back to reality for a bit, although I'm not sure it will feel like reality. My life has been completely transformed."

"Good. I love when that happens." Abby smiled brightly. "Just promise me one thing?"

"What?"

"Don't shut yourself away and hide yourself in that shell again."

"I'll try not to," Tara answered half-heartedly. The truth of the matter was she wasn't quite prepared to make any real promises. Tara wasn't sure she'd be looking for male companionship any time soon. Not that she wanted to be bitter forever, but she felt like she deserved to sit there for a little bit.

"Good girl. I'll be in touch very soon." Abby stood up and gave Tara a big hug. "I think this is the start of a beautiful friendship, my dear."

"Me too."

Tara hugged her back then went to retrieve her bags. Once she got on board the plane, Tara was going to take something to help her sleep. She hoped that the two women she'd flown with the first time didn't join her. That would be the final straw for her.

As Tara made her way to the main building, she heard a voice she didn't want to hear. Rather than acknowledge Ryan, she continued on her way. He didn't let her get much further.

"Tara, we have to talk."

Tara sighed and tried to gather strength somewhere inside her. She channeled some of the anger and turned around to face him. "What do you want, Ryan?"

"I want to explain." His face was covered in guilt.

"There's nothing to talk about, Ryan." Tara shook her head and turned back around.

"Are you leaving?" He asked her.

"Not that it's any of your business, but yes, I'm leaving. There's nothing here for me at the moment."

"Wait, Tara. You can't just go."

"Watch me." Tara continued forward, letting her anger lead her, even though the feelings of betrayal were rising to the surface.

"I'm sorry," his voice was quieter than usual.

"Me too. I should have known better. Que sera. Enjoy your stay, Ryan. I'm sure you'll still have plenty of women who will keep your bed warm."

Tara continued to make her way to the concierge, leaving him where he stood. She didn't even turn around to look at him. She was trying to keep her resolve, and if she saw his handsome face one more time, it would break. Tara could not afford to let that happen.

Checking in with the concierge, she saw Kelli standing nearby. "You leaving, honey?"

"Yes. I need to cut my stay short."

Tara was praying that Kelli would not ask for more details. The woman had been so kind to her before, encouraging her to take a chance. If she hadn't sent her to the mixer, she might never have met Ryan. Even though she was devastated right now, she would still have memories of her time here with him. In time the anger would fade, and hopefully, the memories would not be tainted by the darkness that had been cast over her time.

"Hope it wasn't something here that displeased you."

"Not at all, Kelli. Beau Reve is a beautiful dream, just as you said. I just have reality calling me back. I'll be back again to visit Abby."

"Abby is marvelous. I'm glad you were able to make friends with her." Kelli smiled at her.

"Yes. Well, I've a plane to catch, so I need a ride." Tara didn't want to stay here forever talking about it, especially with Ryan so close by. She just wanted to get out of here as soon as possible.

"I'll have the driver bring the limo by."

Tara sat on the bench in the lobby and waited for her ride. As she sat there, she saw Ryan approaching with his own bags. Tara rolled her eyes and tried to pretend that he wasn't there at all. She had thought the worst-case scenario was the other women. Tara had not factored Ryan into the shared flight equation at all. Thankfully, he didn't say a word but took the bench opposite her.

Part of her was curious as to why he was leaving. Was he heading to work now? Had he already been planning on going? The other half of her didn't really want to know. Tara might not be able to handle the truth. Thankfully, a man came to take her bags and led them to the limousine that was parked out front.

Only two of them got in, Tara and Ryan. She made it a point to look out the window the entire time, ignoring his eyes that seemed to bore holes into her body. As they drove past the beaches, Tara remembered their time on the shore and on the boat. Even though she was extremely pissed off at him, those were memories that touched her even now. It was certainly uncomfortable reliving them with him sitting across from her.

Tara fought the emotions that were battling for control

and tried to keep her face cool and collected. Inside she was a mess, mostly because the cause of her distress was sitting across from her. Why couldn't he have left her alone? She wanted to rip her hair out, poke him in the eyes, pummel her fists in her legs, and smack his face all at the same time. That would just make her look like a toddler throwing a tantrum, and was certainly not the way she wanted to leave the island.

"Are you going to talk to me?"

Tara looked at him and saw the sad smile on his face. "Why?"

"We need to talk, Tara. I need to explain."

She sighed and let the defeat broadcast on her face. "There's nothing you need to explain. We had a good time. You were done. That's all there is to it."

"There's more to it, Tara. So much more." Ryan ran a hand through his hair.

"Just drop it, please. There's nothing to talk about. We both knew this was a temporary thing."

"I didn't mean to hurt you, Tara." His voice was sincere.

"You didn't," she lied.

"I looked for you last night."

After he had slept with another woman, publicly, when he had said he was away on business. Tara didn't have much to say to that, except hammer the nail into the coffin a little more. "I had a date. Jake. Sexy, dark haired, big biceps. And there was Phillip the night before. Never knew how attractive a bald man could be. I think I kind of like that."

Her remarks had hit home. Ryan seemed quite distressed by her words. "I see. I thought you were waiting for me."

"Well, isn't that a pity." Her voice was dripping with honey. "Like I said, there's nothing to explain. We're good."

"Then, why are you leaving?" He clearly wasn't believing her.

"I have to get to work." Which was true in a way. Not that she'd be returning to the night club like he probably assumed. She was curious as to why he was leaving but did not really want to know the reason.

"I think you work too hard." He shook his head.

"That's life. We don't all have the luxury to come and go as we please." Her words hit home.

"That's not fair, Tara. I've worked hard for every penny I earned."

"I know you have. It's what I admired about you." At least she used to. Her admiration had changed the minute he had lied to her.

"And then?"

Tara looked away from him. "I woke up."

Ryan didn't say another word, and she refused to look at him. It was too soon, and she was nursing a pain that she could not vocalize to him. She had no right to be so attached to him. He wasn't looking for a relationship, and

Tara hadn't realized that she was until it was too late to keep herself from getting attached. He'd never know the love she hid deep inside, and that was for the best.

The minute they got on the airplane, Tara took some of her sleeping pills and prayed for them to kick in. As she fell asleep, her mind was plagued with memories she would never be able to shove deep inside her. His hands all over her body, his mouth making love to her most intimate places, the way he seemed to master every inch of her. Tara's dreams were plagued with memories that only made her wish she could keep him near.

When she awoke, her face was flushed. She saw Ryan watching her from his seat across from her. Looking away, she looked at her phone and realized that she had only managed to get eight hours of sleep. That meant she still had ten hours to go. She swiveled her chair so that she wasn't facing him any longer and put a hand to her cheeks. Definitely flushed. Good grief, how was she going to get through the rest of this flight without embarrassing herself further? The problem wasn't just her face. Her entire body was on fire, longing for the memory to become a reality one last time, but Tara could not give in to that.

Ryan must have realized that talking to her was not something that would get him anywhere. There was nowhere to go. Their time together was over. All she had to do now as get through this flight without speaking to him further. A little self-control and distraction that didn't make her feel like jumping his bones would be the only thing that would get her through. She thumbed through the movie selection before her and put a pair of headphones over her ears. The time moved a little faster than a turtle's pace, but not by much.

Chapter 19

Thankfully, Tara was able to disembark the plane with very little interaction with Ryan. She didn't want a long drawn out goodbye. When she collected her bags, she saw him at the baggage claim.

"Still not talking to me?" He asked her softly.

"What is left to say, Ryan? Have a nice life. Thank you for the memories."

His face was filled with regret as she turned away from him, but Tara could not deal with that right now. Every inch of her was fighting the urge to throw herself in his arms. Tara knew that was a horrible idea. That would only end up in further heartbreak. From here, it was going to be hard enough to pick up the pieces.

As she walked away, she fought the tears that threatened to fall down her face. "Pull it together, Tara."

Thankfully, no one seemed to notice her talking to

herself. When she turned around, she saw that Ryan had already disappeared. That was probably a good thing. No more temptation to pull back in. Smooth sailing from here on out. At least that's what she told herself.

Tara texted for a driver and waited for the taxi to come to pick her up. As she did, she sent a message to Amelia to let her know she was on her way home. Then she shut off her phone because inevitably her friend would message her back, wanting to know why she was coming home so early. Tara did not have the energy to explain right now. In fact, now that she'd sent the message, she wished there was some way to instantly retract it. Why had she done that?

The ride home was fairly quiet. Maybe the driver realized that she was not in a talkative mood. She was thankful for that, and actually tipped him more. Tara remained lost in thought on the way home. She tried to distract herself from Ryan with all the business plans she would have to come up with for Coquette. There was a lot of work to do. As much as she tried to think about where to start, her mind always traveled back to the last time she had seen his face. Regret. She understood that. She was having plenty of those, but hers centered around why she had let him get to her in the first place. Tara had known better.

While she had left Beau Reve a little heartbroken, she was still a braver woman than when she had first arrived. She owed that to Ryan. No matter how angry she was at him, she could still admit that. He had created memories that she would never forget. Some day they would be less tarnished. Right now, she was just feeling the raw aftereffects of the lie he had told so easily.

When they pulled into the drive, she saw that Amelia's car was parked on the street before the house. Amelia was waiting impatiently for her on her porch. She quickly dealt with getting her bags and thanked the driver for the ride.

Tara opened the garage and gestured for her to come inside. "What are you doing here?"

"Well, you texted me that you were coming home early. I am dying to know how the trip went." Amelia looked as if she were ready for Tara to gush and spill the beans.

Tara opened her door and ushered Amelia inside. "Come on in."

"So?"

Tara let her luggage slide to the floor and shook her head at her. "What do you want to know?"

"Did you get laid?"

"Really, that's the first thing you're leading with?" Tara blushed, unable to deflect the way that she hoped she would be able to.

"Yes, of course, it is. Have you met me?" She shook her head at Tara.

"Right. Yes. And just one man. He was…. Well, he was fantastic…at first."

"Uh-uh. There's more to it." Amelia's gaze probed hers.

"I don't want to talk about it." Tara shook her head

and looked away. She didn't want Amelia to know she had fallen in love with a man in an impossible situation in just a week's time.

"Oh, dear. You've got it bad. Did you get his number?"

"He's a billionaire, Amelia. He probably has twenty girls on the side. He sure had a handful on the island."

"That's probably true. Ah well. At least now you can say you had a fling. Every girl needs one."

"If you say so. He's probably ruined me for life, though." Tara closed her eyes and sighed longingly.

"Wow, he was good."

"He seduced me, Amelia. Made me feel like the only woman he was interested in. It was great the first few days. And when we finally did sleep together, two days or so of it, he told me he had to go to work, but he would be back." Tara felt her eyes water slightly and tried to push the emotions away from her.

"But?"

"Abby took me to a peep show the second day—"

"You went to a peep show? Holy hell! Good girl…. Oh, sorry. Continue."

"He was on display with another woman."

"When he said he had to go to work?" Amelia's face turned to disgust. "Asshole."

"Exactly. He didn't have to lie to me. Hell, he didn't have to weave his spell around me the way he did. He could have been honest."

"Yeah, that's bullshit. Men who lie—there are far too many of them."

"Truth!" Tara sighed. "It was good, though, Amelia. The best ever. I've never been so free. And the best part is, I know what I am going to do for the rest of my life."

"If you're going to become an escort, I'll have to stop you right there." Amelia held up a hand and pointed a finger at her.

"What? No! When I was there, I told Abby what I do. In just three days, she created a plan to make a night club that she wants me to run. It's going to be amazing. And the best part is that the goal is to treat our servers like high-class women."

"So, no ass grabbing?"

"Exactly! And no slutty outfits. Classy. Refined. I'm hoping I can steal you away from Lane when it opens."

"Girl, you had me at no ass grabbing. Half the girls would come with you in a heartbeat."

"So, my life is changing in so many ways. And that's thanks to you. For recommending Beau Reve and for encouraging me to give it a try."

"That's awesome, Tara! I'm so happy for you. You deserve to be happy. I just wish you didn't have to leave on account of some dickweed."

"Me too, Amelia. But it's as much my fault as his. I knew there were no strings, and I fell for him anyway."

"You love him?" Amelia asked her.

"Yes. At least I would have. I'm not really sure how I feel right now."

The doorbell rang, and they both looked at each other. "Huh...I wonder if I left something in the taxi."

"I'll come with you, just in case there's some stalker out there."

The two of them walked to the door, Tara rolling her eyes at her overdramatic friend who was brandishing an umbrella in her hand like a sword.

Tara opened the door and found Ryan standing in her doorway. Tara thought she was seeing things. "What are you doing here?"

"Wait...this is the guy?" Amelia was clearly surprised.

"Yes, and why?"

"Hello again. Amelia, right?" Ryan greeted her.

"Oh, God...did you sleep with him too?" Tara put a hand to her head and wanted to sink somewhere far beneath the ground.

"No!" Two voices answered at the same time. Ryan was defensive as he held his hands in front of him. Amelia had a look on her face like she wished she'd had the chance, but she quickly guarded her face.

"How do you know each other?"

Ryan looked over at Amelia and shook his head, but Amelia rolled her eyes. "I'm not doing you any favors, you prick. He was the one who came to the club, Tara."

"I'm not a prick—" Ryan tried to defend himself.

"Wait...you were the one who put my name in to Beau Reve? Did you pay for me too?" Tara was starting to feel even more like a prostitute than she had before.

"No, no, I didn't. Have them fax over the details if you don't believe me."

"Why should I believe you?"

"Yeah, jackass...why should she believe you?"

Tara turned to Amelia and gave her a chillout look. "Amelia, can we talk tomorrow?"

"What, and leave you here with him?" Amelia crossed her arms over her chest.

"He may be many things, but he is not a serial killer. He's not going to hurt me." Not physically, at least. Emotionally she had already been shattered the minute he showed up on her doorstep. There was no denying that.

"Fine. But if you don't text me in a little while to tell me you're safe, I'll be calling the cops."

As Amelia left, she split her fingers and pointed at her eyes, then turned them around on Ryan as if to tell him she was watching him.

Tara closed the door behind Amelia and turned around to face Ryan. "Why are you here?"

"You left before I could say goodbye."

"Oh. Is that all? Well, goodbye." Tara pointed to the door.

"I need to explain myself."

"Fine. What do you want to talk about, Ryan?" Tara

led him to the living room and sat down on the armchair to listen to his explanation. She was actually fairly tired, so she hoped he got to the point soon.

"I lied to you."

"Really?" She snorted. "You think?"

"I didn't have to go to work. I just needed time."

"To sleep with other women. You didn't have to lie about that."

"I didn't sleep with anyone."

"Okay, Bill...I suppose she has a blue dress in her closet somewhere too." He had to be all presidential, didn't he?

"I wanted to."

"Yes, I was pretty sure your erection showed that pretty well for you." Tara shook her head and started to rub her temples.

"No...not like that. I'm really screwing this up."

"Nowhere to go but up from here. But even then, you'd have trouble climbing out of the hole you dug."

"I was trying to erase you. You invaded my thoughts, Tara, in ways no woman ever has before."

"Oh, this should be good." She tapped a finger on her knees, knowing that she was only half-listening to what he had to say.

"From the beginning, when I saw you in the club, I was drawn to you, Tara. When you accepted the invitation to Beau Reve, I thought I might have a chance to figure out what it was that made you so unique."

Tara crossed her arms over her chest. "So, you looked for me?"

"I did."

"This whole time, it wasn't a matter of chance, but an arrangement. You wanted to fuck me out of your system."

"No…. Yes…. I don't know. The point is, it didn't work. No woman has ever had this pull over me."

Tara sighed and looked away from him. "I hate you for saying that."

"I know, and I deserve it. I wasn't looking for love, Tara, but I can't deny how I feel for you any longer."

"Love?" Her voice sounded haunted. Why would he say those words to her? Tears sprang to her eyes, and she fought the urge to throw something at him. "Why are you screwing with me, Ryan?"

"I love you, Tara. I know I've screwed up, but I just want a chance to make it right. Please look at me," he pleaded with her.

Tara was afraid to look at him, but she did it anyway. His face was haunted as if he carried a deep pain inside him. "I can't do this. What if you suddenly decide I'm not enough, Ryan? Will you go running to Beau Reve? Will you find someone else to sleep with? Will you lie to me again?"

"I'm imperfect. I'm learning to be better, but as long as we're together, I promise there will be no one but you."

"Was there anyone else on the island?" Tara asked him.

"No. Besides the peep show, no, and even that ended

right after you left."

"She must have been disappointed." Tara could relate. He had strung her along for a few days.

"I'm not on her list of people she wants to talk to at the moment, not that it matters. The only one I want is you. If you'll have me."

"What do you mean, Ryan?"

"I'm ready for the next step in my life, Tara. I'm looking for someone to build a future with. I think we could do very well together."

"I see." Tara still refused to give in to the thoughts racing through her head. Had he said he loved her? How was that possible? It didn't make sense, but some things weren't meant to. Considering how she felt for him, she could understand the rush of feelings inside him. She felt it too.

"Tara...." He looked as if he were trying to find another way to persuade her, but her lack of response to his words was visibly tearing him apart.

"You broke my heart, Ryan."

"I know," he whispered as he got to his knees before her. "And I'd spend a lifetime making up for it, if you let me. I love you, Tara."

She closed her eyes, and a few tears fell down her cheeks. Ryan kissed them away, which only made her want to cry even harder. He gathered her in his arms and held her close, stroking her hair.

When she stopped crying, Tara finally looked him deep in the eyes. She saw the love hidden deep inside and put her hand on his cheek. "I love you too, Ryan."

His mouth came down to hers and kissed her softly, so delicate she barely registered the kiss. "I promise to be a better man."

"Good, because I'm going to need your help with a new business. I'm pretty sure Abby wouldn't mind if you helped out." She wrinkled her nose at him.

"We already have a meeting scheduled for a few weeks."

"Abby!" She shook her head. "Matchmaking all the way?"

"She's a diehard romantic."

Tara snuggled against him. "You're mine, Ryan. Got that?"

"Yes, ma'am." He kissed the top of her head. "I wouldn't have it any other way."

Ever since childhood, Elissa Daye has enjoyed reading stories as an escape from life. When she was a teenager, she started to write her own stories that kept her entertained when she ran out of books to read. When she was accepted into Illinois Summer School for the Arts in her Junior year of High School, she knew she wanted to become a writer. Elissa graduated from Illinois State University in December 1999 with a Bachelor of Science in Elementary Education and began her teaching career, hoping to find moments to write in her free time.

After seven years of teaching, Elissa decided to focus on her writing and made the decision to put her teaching years behind her so that she could create the stories she had always dreamed of. She is now happily married and a stay at home mom, who writes in every spare moment she can find, doing her best to master the art of multitasking to get everything accomplished.